PUFFI

THE ASSASSIN N

Manisha Anand grew up in a tiny place in central India that no one ever bothered to put on a map, where she had several imaginary friends and read far too many books. She now lives in a tiny house in London with a lovely Northern chap, their imaginary cat and a growing collection of books that is threatening to take over. She thinks life's turned out quite all right.

THE ASSASSIN NUNS OF PISTACHIO

MANISHA ANAND

ILLUSTRATIONS BY
SUKANTO DEBNATH

PUFFIN BOOKS

PUFFIN BOOKS
Published by the Penguin Group
Penguin Books India Pvt. Ltd, 7th Floor, Infinity Tower C, DLF Cyber City, Gurgaon 122 002, Haryana, India
Penguin Group (USA) Inc., 375 Hudson Street, New York, New York 10014, USA
Penguin Group (Canada), 90 Eglinton Avenue East, Suite 700, Toronto, Ontario, M4P 2Y3, Canada
Penguin Books Ltd, 80 Strand, London WC2R 0RL, England
Penguin Ireland, 25 St Stephen's Green, Dublin 2, Ireland (a division of Penguin Books Ltd)
Penguin Group (Australia), 707 Collins Street, Melbourne, Victoria 3008, Australia
Penguin Group (NZ), 67 Apollo Drive, Rosedale, Auckland 0632, New Zealand
Penguin Books (South Africa) (Pty) Ltd, Block D, Rosebank Office Park, 181 Jan Smuts Avenue, Parktown North, Johannesburg 2193, South Africa

Penguin Books Ltd, Registered Offices: 80 Strand, London WC2R 0RL, England

First published in Puffin by Penguin Books India 2015

10 9 8 7 6 5 4 3 2 1

ISBN 9780143333654

Typeset in Minion Pro by Manipal Digital Systems, Manipal
Printed at Thomson Press India Ltd, New Delhi

A PENGUIN RANDOM HOUSE COMPANY

For my parents

I had a fabulous childhood, so here's a book about nuns who love swords and cake. I think it's a fair swap.

Prologue

It was a bright and sunny afternoon as the Assassin Nuns of Pistachio headed back up to their mountaintop abbey after yet another successful mission. They clambered up the mountain, single file, wearing an assortment of armour and weapons that they were slowly removing to reveal simple black and white robes held in place with brown braided belts.

'That was an excellent day's work, sisters!' the Mother Superior said cheerfully, putting her sword back into its sheath and tucking a stray lock of grey hair into her wimple. 'Absolutely amazing.' The sunlight glinted off her chain mail as she beamed at the other nuns. 'That's the nine hundred and fifty-fifth problem we've solved since we've been here,' she continued proudly. 'And today was yet another wonderful example of teamwork and—'

'Well, maybe not completely wonderful,' Sister Gilbertine said slowly, taking her elbow guards off and putting them into a bag. 'We did initially blow up the wrong house when Sister Portia gave the order to fire.' She pulled her gloves off one at a time and stuffed them in, holding the bag under one arm as she zipped it shut.

'I didn't mean to!' Sister Portia said as she hurried to keep up with the others. 'I thought it was the right one, but my eyes aren't as good as they used to be. Regular everyday buildings and evil headquarters look the same to me now.' She took her glasses off and shook her head at them ruefully. 'I think there's something wrong with my glasses.'

'There's nothing wrong with your glasses,' Sister Gilbertine said firmly. 'I think we're all just getting a little too old for this.'

'But it all turned out fine in the end,' Sister Portia persisted, shoving her glasses up the bridge of her nose. 'That house ended up being one where the pirates of Wolf Rock held their mid-month plotting sessions, so we did manage to prevent a lot of high seas plundering.'

'We were just lucky this time,' Sister Gilbertine said, shaking her head. 'Maybe we should hold off on any more attacks until we're sure we won't be making any more mistakes.'

'But I like blowing things up,' Sister Portia said sadly, looking down at the spare sticks of dynamite in her pocket. 'It's ever so much fun!'

'A lot of fun,' Sister Mildew piped in as she kicked her shin guards off.

'Maybe Sister Gilbertine is right,' sighed the Mother Superior, reaching down to pick up a stray piece of armour as it rolled past her. 'Maybe we're not as young as we used to be. I didn't want to say anything while we were in the middle of a swordfight, but I'm starting to find my weapon a bit too heavy to wield sometimes.'

'My eyes aren't quite the same either,' Sister Regina said, stopping to squint down her shotgun. 'I'm sure I saw something stuck inside here and now it won't come out.' She blew into the barrel of the gun and grimaced as a cloud of dust and gunpowder blew out. 'Ugh,' she said, brushing flecks of dirt off her face.

'Sister Regina, would you kindly be more careful with your firearm?' The Mother Superior peered over at her, concerned. 'We don't want another little accident like last week.'

'I wasn't really going to shoot old Mrs Hastings,' Sister Regina retorted indignantly, tucking her weapon into her belt. 'I meant to point my umbrella at her, not my gun. It's an easy enough mistake to make.'

Sister Gilbertine frowned. 'I'm not sure it's that easy a mis—'

'I think my hearing's starting to go a little funny,' Sister Kiki said thoughtfully. 'When the Mother Superior yelled "Attack!" earlier, I thought she was saying "Snack!" and got distracted looking for my bag of fruit.' She pulled an apple out of her pocket and wiped it down her sleeve before taking a hearty bite out of it. 'I was awfully confused when everyone started charging.'

'The Most Reverend Mother up north did say they had replacements in mind for when we were ready to leave,' the Mother Superior said reluctantly. 'A whole set of new nuns who can take over and continue the work we're doing here.'

'It's just my glasses,' Sister Portia said half-heartedly. 'I'm sure they just don't work any more, it's all fine.' The nuns continued on their way in a pensive silence, with Sister Regina ambling along at the rear, still curiously peering down the barrel of her shotgun.

'Have you ever thought about what you're going to go after you retire?' Sister Kiki asked as they got to the top of the mountain. 'I think I'd like to live somewhere near a beach.'

'I'm moving to a quiet little place where nothing ever happens,' Sister Portia said. 'Somewhere small and insignificant that has no crime and no trouble whatsoever.'

'Oh, I'm settling in a city,' the Mother Superior said firmly. 'Everything bad seems to happen in small towns. I want a nice, big sprawling city where no one knows my name and where they have the police to take care of their problems.' She smiled wistfully into the distance. 'I would love to finish reading a book without being interrupted by bandits driving through the town and putting everyone's life in peril.'

'Retiring? Who's retiring?' Sister Mildew looked around sharply.

'We're all retiring,' Sister Regina replied patiently. 'We're getting too old.'

'Nonsense,' Sister Mildew said, wrapping her arms around her sword. 'I'm never leaving.'

'But you wandered away in the middle of the fight today to catch a butterfly,' Sister Regina persisted, as Sister Mildew ignored her and marched onwards to the abbey. 'You forgot we were fighting!'

'It was a good fight, though, wasn't it?' Sister Kiki smiled at the others. 'A burning building full of cutlass-wielding buccaneers. I think it's been my favourite so far.'

'Really?' Sister Regina laughed. 'My favourite was definitely the time the band of marauders set up camp outside town and tried to steal Farmer Askew's sheep. Remember how we had to climb up to the bell tower and shoot them without injuring the livestock?' She patted her quiver of arrows affectionately. 'All twelve of those nasty thieves knocked down and not a scratch on a single lamb.'

'Oh, that was nothing,' Sister Gilbertine waved her hand dismissively. 'The battle against the League of Unfriendly Ninjas in the cornfield was surely one of our finest moments. Besides, we ended up accidentally harvesting most of the crop that day with all the swords flying about and Farmer Crinkleberry was so pleased.'

The nuns stood outside the front gate, looking through the iron bars at their abbey. 'I can't believe we've been here for forty years,' Sister Portia said softly. 'I do hope the next set of nuns who come here love this job as much as we do.'

'I think the new nun will stay on to lead the others,' the Mother Superior looked thoughtfully at the abbey.

'Although I've noticed that she always seems to find an excuse to remain at the abbey when it's time to go out and fight.'

'She told me the other day that she finds dealing with danger uncomfortable,' Sister Kiki announced.

'Danger?' Sister Portia scowled. 'I laugh in the face of danger!' She waved her sword in the air, narrowly missing Sister Gilbertine's head.

'Sister Portia!' Sister Gilbertine cried, ducking just in time.

'Oh, I'm awfully sorry,' Sister Portia said, putting her sword away. 'I didn't see you there. I told you there was something wrong with my glasses.'

'How are they going to pick our replacements, anyway?' Sister Kiki asked curiously. 'It's quite a special sort of job we do here. It's not for everyone.'

'I'm never leaving,' Sister Mildew repeated stubbornly.

'I think they use forms,' the Mother Superior said vaguely, scratching her chin. 'Lots of research and official forms. It's an organized way of getting things done.'

'I filled out a form when they gave me these glasses,' Sister Portia said, tucking the offending article into her pocket as she unlatched the gate and headed down the gravel path to the front door. 'I filled out a form nice and clear, and look how that turned out.' She turned to glance at the other nuns as she pulled the house keys out of her pocket. 'It didn't turn out very well at all.'

1

This story starts, like any good story does, far, far away and in a tiny town you've never heard of before.

Named affectionately for the surrounding mountains that were covered in trees of a most peculiar shade of green, the little town of Pistachio sat nestled away from the noise and clamour of the rest of the world, perfectly content with itself. The people were friendly, peaceful and enjoyed a good cup of tea while waiting for their crops to grow, and the place was quaint and beautiful, much like a picture postcard. It was the sort of town where nothing much ever happened, but which was quite sleepily satisfied with its lack of excitement.

While Pistachio itself wasn't much of a tourist destination, it was well known for its wonderful produce. Traders made their way here every month for the local market day, their trucks filled with crates of exotic vegetables and unpronounceable delicacies to swap for the locals' wonderful cornbread, ripe cheese and strawberry preserves. Every year, during the town's Summer and

Winter Festivals, market day was extra special, with competitions ranging from growing the shiniest apple to knitting the most elaborate jumper, along with plenty of chocolate fountains, brightly painted clowns and rousing renditions of ballads around a bonfire in the evenings.

It was the morning of one such Summer Festival when Farmer Argyll filled his battered grey van with fresh ears of corn and sat his robust pig, Horace, wrapped snugly in a pig-sized tartan scarf, on the passenger seat next to him.

'You alright there, Horace?' he asked proudly, carefully placing the seat belt around his beloved pet.

Farmer Argyll certainly had every right to be proud. Over the last few months, he had been raising Horace for one purpose and one purpose alone: to win the blue ribbon at the Pistachio Perfect Pig Competition, a prize that had eluded him for four years. Determined to add this one missing award to his sagging shelf of trophies this year, Farmer Argyll had done everything he possibly could to ensure that they won. He'd stayed up late reading books on pig care and nourishment, carefully writing out meal plans and driving his wife crazy by cooking Horace's dinners in her spotless kitchen, but it seemed like his efforts had finally paid off. Horace was a spectacular specimen, with giant haunches that rolled when he walked and an air of impeccable charm that his owner was convinced none of the other pigs would have.

'You're a winner, old boy,' he stated, scratching the pig behind its enormous ear. 'You're an absolute winner.' Horace grunted dismissively. He was very aware of the fact that he was a winner, but he was also hungry and his breakfast bucket of potato peelings, carrots and grapes hadn't quite filled him up.

The sun peered out through the clouds as the farmer and his pig drove into Pistachio, one cheerfully optimistic and the other fast asleep. The town square was being set up with dozens of wooden stalls between the bell tower and the mayor's office, and Mr Pratt, the local electrician, was balanced on a very tall ladder, stringing colourful bunting along the trees. 'Looking sharp there, Horace,' Mr Pratt shouted down as Farmer Argyll drove past, but Horace was too busy dreaming of cake to notice.

A few council members who had managed to wake up early on a Saturday morning wandered around aimlessly, offering (mostly unhelpful) advice as the farmers and traders piled their wares up and swapped stories over steaming cups of tea. Further up, a breakfast barbecue had been fired up and the morning air was filled with the pleasant and heady combination of bacon and melted cheese. A handful of townspeople had already started trickling in under the giant banner that read 'Pistachio's 56th Summer Festival!' in bright red letters. Everyone in the town had a particular stall they preferred, and no one wanted to miss out on a slice of their favourite pie because they'd dawdled while getting out of bed.

As morning turned into noon, people showed no signs of slowing down. The sun shone down brightly as families milled around the town square, clutching balloons, sausages and giant teddy bears with great enthusiasm. A group of men were strumming guitars and children joined in, singing loudly as they waved sticks of bright pink cotton candy.

'It's a mighty fine day for a festival,' Mrs Allsop said, sniffing at a peach from the fruit stand and trying to balance her baby on her hip. 'It's so much better than last year's terrible rain-soaked effort. Poor Emmy caught a terrible cold and we were so worried.'

Mrs Skillet nodded in agreement, arranging her wares in bushel-sized baskets and reaching out to grab a pair of scissors from an inquisitive Emmy, who promptly blew a spit bubble in displeasure.

'Think any of those nuns will make it down this year?' Mrs Allsop gestured in the vague direction of the mountain.

Mrs Skillet shrugged. 'I haven't seen any of them for quite a few years now. Last time one of them was down, it was to trade some of their tomatoes for a couple of pork chops, I think.'

'I hear they grow some lovely vegetables up there on the mountain,' Mrs Allsop said. 'All sorts of fancy things that just won't grow down here. All we ever grow in our garden is cucumbers. We like our cucumbers, though, don't we, Emmy?' Emmy blew another spit bubble. She preferred cake to cucumbers.

'Aye, but they used to come down here a lot more,' said Mrs Skillet. 'Back in the day, they used to come down every Sunday for an after-church lunch with the mayor once they were done getting rid of any unsavoury characters around.'

'Didn't they once rescue old Mrs Nobbit and her granddaughter from the hot-air balloon bandits?' Mrs Allsop asked, picking an apple up and eyeing it appraisingly.

'They did?' Mrs Skillet looked uncertain.

'You went to school with the girl for a while, you must have heard about that,' Mrs Allsop said. 'Little Jade was playing in the garden, just as nice as can be, when a rope ladder drops down and a man holding a cutlass in his teeth climbs down and grabs her. Old Mrs Nobbit came rushing at them, but he grabbed her as well and took them both up to the balloon.'

'What on earth did they want with an old lady and a little girl?' Mrs Skillet looked unconvinced.

'Who knows,' Mrs Allsop said, fussing over Emmy. 'Some people just like to kidnap for no reason.'

'Did the nuns shoot the balloon down?' Mrs Skillet asked.

'No, they shot a grapping hook up and tied the other end to a tree,' Mrs Allsop replied. 'Then they all climbed up to the balloon, one after the other, shooting arrows the whole time. They had excellent aim; they hit everyone but old Mrs Nobbit and little Jade. By the time they got up to the basket, all the bandits were out

cold and old Mrs Nobbit was clobbering the awful men over the head with her walking stick.'

'I do remember hearing about that now,' Mrs Skillet said with a laugh. 'They called them the Flying Nuns that day.'

'That would be way back before Emmy was born,' Mrs Allsop remarked. 'Before I started teaching at the school as well. I remember them being around all the time, popping in to say hello and helping with the market-day madness.'

'Those would have been different nuns back then,' Mrs Skillet said, admiring a basket of particularly ripe cherries. 'They were coming on quite old and I reckon they've all been replaced now. The new ones haven't been to see us at all.' She wrinkled her nose as she thought. 'Been about fifteen years now, I think?'

Mrs Allsop unscrewed a jar of baby food and tried coaxing a spoonful into Emmy's mouth. Emmy stared suspiciously at the orange goop and shook her head firmly. 'They've had their invitation again like every year—Susie from the council office says she sent it up this week.' Mrs Allsop lowered her voice and leaned in closer. 'I also heard that Mr Smythe tried bringing up a discussion about them signing the town charter again and maybe visiting us more often, but they never replied.'

Mrs Skillet laughed disdainfully. 'Oh, they'll never come down here,' she said. They think they're too good for us with their fancy mountaintop abbey.'

'I talked to one of them once last year,' Mrs Allsop said absently. 'I was out for a walk and wandered past the path that leads up to the abbey. One of the nuns was down there waiting for the bus to drop off a visitor. She seemed a bit afraid of everything, if you ask me. Jumping at every sound she heard.' Mrs Allsop waved her spoon in Emmy's face. 'Come on, darling, don't be fussy. Carrots are very good for you! Emmy darling?' The baby's attention, however, had been diverted, like that of most of the people milling about. A shiny black car had just come in through the square, causing the general hubbub to stop temporarily.

There weren't many shiny black cars that ever stopped at Pistachio. As a matter of fact, a shiny black car had never stopped anywhere near Pistachio. Nothing but battered vans, bicycles and the occasional bus ever passed through. People tried not to stare as a tall, pale man in a dark overcoat stepped out of the car, slamming the door behind him with a firm hand.

'Who's that then?' Mrs Allsop whispered, taking advantage of the distraction to stuff the spoonful of creamed carrots into Emmy's mouth.

Mrs Skillet shrugged, as she was fond of doing. 'I've never seen him before in my life.'

'Maybe he's lost his way,' Mrs Allsop said. 'No one with a car like that would ever come here.'

'No, I don't think he's lost,' said Mrs Skillet. 'He seems to know Mr Smythe.'

The deputy mayor was indeed headed towards the strange man, a broad smile on his face and his arm outstretched. The council members crowded behind him as the two men shook hands and shared a polite laugh. After introducing him to the others, the deputy mayor gestured towards the preparations for the town festival and directed the stranger towards the stalls.

'He doesn't look like a tourist,' decided Mrs Allsop. 'Not that we ever get any tourists. My cousin Millie from up north, she gets a proper load of tourists every summer. Those ones dressed in shorts, wandering around with those fancy phones and talking maps in their cars.'

'Expensive car,' sniffed Mrs Skillet. She rearranged her fruit, keeping an eye on the deputy mayor and his strange new acquaintance.

'I haven't been in a real fancy car since I was a little girl,' Mrs Allsop said wistfully. 'I suppose there's no real use having one over here, with all the mud and fields.'

'Nowhere really to go either,' pointed out Mrs Skillet. 'It looks like they're coming this way,' she added in a low voice. 'Maybe we should just—'

'Mrs Skillet!' The deputy mayor made his way towards the fruit stand, with the man in the dark coat behind him.

Mrs Skillet straightened out her apron and smiled politely. 'Hello there, Mr Smythe. How can I help you today?'

'This is Mrs Skillet,' the deputy mayor said to the man, waving at the general direction of the fruit stall. 'She's from the farm at the edge of the town and her peaches are simply beyond compare.' He picked one up and handed it to him with a flourish.

The stranger sniffed at the peach and smiled. It was hard to tell how old he was, and both women would later swear he could have easily been either twenty or sixty. His face was pale and sallow and his shiny black hair was slicked back neatly over a rather oddly-shaped skull. 'I am inclined to believe you,' he said to Mr Smythe, his voice deep and not altogether pleasant. He took a bite of the fruit, pausing to dab at the sides of his mouth gently with a white handkerchief. 'Divine.'

'This is Mr Knight,' Mr Smythe explained to the women. 'He's here to invest in Pistachio.'

'Invest in Pistachio?' Mrs Skillet repeated in surprise, unable to tear her eyes away from Mr Knight. She suppressed a shudder as the man continued to slowly eat her peach.

The deputy mayor laughed nervously. 'He's helping us rebuild our economy and get things on track. We've been very lucky; he's told me all about the wonderful things he's done for the other towns he's helped out.'

'Pistachio will be back on the map,' Mr Knight said, dropping the peach pit on the ground and drying his fingers on his handkerchief. 'This town will soon be running the way it was meant to, with no frivolities and waste of resources.'

'I think we've been doing fine,' Mrs Allsop interjected, shifting a fidgeting Emmy from one arm to the other. 'We're a small town but we like it that way.'

Mr Knight smiled widely. 'A small town is simply a big town that hasn't grown up yet.' He cleared his throat as if to elaborate, but before he could go any further, the sound of excited voices and a pig's squeal interrupted him.

'Oh dear,' said Mr Smythe, turning around. 'What's all this commotion now?'

The commotion was exactly what a well-deserved victory sounded like. While the deputy mayor and his new acquaintance had been sampling local produce and meeting the townspeople, the Pistachio Perfect Pig Competition had finally come to an end, with Horace crowned as the rightful winner. A very delighted Farmer Argyll had then proceeded to parade Horace around, much to the pig's dismay. Horace had cared nothing for the blue ribbon or the shiny medal—if anything wasn't edible, he simply wasn't interested. He proceeded to show his indignation by knocking over any display within reach of his snout, resulting in much scrambling around and shouting as people tried to keep their wares from being trampled on.

Mr Knight's eyes narrowed in displeasure. 'Why is there a pig wandering around in the market?'

'Oh, don't worry, that's just from the pig competition,' Mr Smythe waved dismissively. 'There's a pie-eating contest soon as well—that's always a good one!' He started to walk towards a colourful tent festooned with plastic fruit and motioned at the stranger to follow him.

'What purpose do all these competitions serve?' Mr Knight asked, his voice still tinged with disapproval.

Mrs Allsop laughed. 'Oh, there's no real purpose there, mister. They just help keep people happy. Lord knows we all need a good laugh every now and then.'

Mr Knight pursed his lips, clearly disagreeing with her. 'We should take our leave, there's much to talk about,' he said, giving the deputy mayor a meaningful glance. 'It was a pleasure meeting you, ladies.' He leaned towards Emmy. 'And you too, child.' Emmy took the opportunity to spit the offending mouthful of carrot out, and her aim was spot on.

'I'm ever so sorry!' Mrs Allsop looked through her pockets for a tissue, but Mr Knight waved her away. Wiping his face with his handkerchief, he gave the women a curt nod and left, followed closely by an apologetic Mr Smythe.

'I don't think Emmy likes the new man,' Mrs Allsop said, fussing over her baby. 'She's making the same face she does when she's seen a spider.'

'I think Emmy's a wise one,' said Mrs Skillet thoughtfully, watching the men head towards the mayor's office.

And later events would prove that Emmy really was.

2

One year later

While Mr Knight's mysterious arrival in Pistachio was only the beginning of very bad things indeed, somewhere on top of the mountain that towered over the little town, nap time was just coming to an end at the abbey that housed Pistachio's Assassin Nuns.

The abbey was a beautiful old stone house, with a jumble of rose bushes and vegetable plots on either side. A mass of ivy grew stubbornly up one side of the front of the house, giving it an almost rakish appearance, and the building was surrounded by tall trees, whose bark and branches were the same pale green as their waxy leaves.

A gust of wind blew in through an open window on the first floor, brushing the curtains aside and blowing a pile of papers across the wooden floor. A tall round-faced woman clad in grey opened her eyes, readjusted her wimple and yawned in dismay as she looked at the time. The large white clock on the wall next to a picture of an overly cheerful saint clearly stated that afternoon prayers should have started twenty minutes ago.

'Sister Agnes!' she yelled, jumping out of bed and scrambling for the papers on the floor. She fastened the window and reached for her prayer beads. 'Sister Agnes, I asked you to wake me!' she said, shutting the door to her room firmly behind her, pausing for a second to realign the sign on it that said 'The Reverend Mother'.

After a quick knock on the door next to hers, she poked her head into Sister Agnes's room, only to discover that her second-in-command, too, had fallen asleep. The Reverend Mother coughed politely. Sister Agnes woke up and sat bolt upright in her chair. 'I'm awake,' she said quickly, turning a page of the book in her hand. 'Did you want me for anything, Reverend Mother?'

'We missed afternoon prayers,' the Reverend Mother said, tapping her foot impatiently. 'That's the second time that's happened this week.'

'Oh dear, not again!' Sister Agnes said, reaching for her hymn book with one hand and her shoes with the other. 'I was just going to shut my eyes for one minute, I really was.'

'Well, come along,' the Reverend Mother said. 'Let's be on our way. The rest of them will be waiting in the chapel.' The two women made their way hurriedly down the stairs, trying to wipe the sleep from their eyes. They turned around the corner and headed to the old chapel door, expecting to hear the voices of five nuns singing hymns, but were greeted with the sight of a locked door and a deserted hallway instead.

'I don't think we were the only ones to oversleep,' Sister Agnes observed, suppressing a yawn.

The Reverend Mother sighed and shook her head. 'We really need to stop having such large breakfasts.'

***

Later that evening, seven nuns sat around a wooden table, surrounded by the remains of a hearty dinner. Sister Ruth came in from the kitchen and passed around helpings of strawberry crumble for dessert. She placed the generously filled bowls in front of each nun and put a jug of cream on the table. 'Help yourself,' she said with a bright smile. 'Not my best effort, though,' she added apologetically. 'Next time I might use more cinnamon.'

Sister Ruth was a small, dumpling-shaped woman who was on an endless quest to invent the perfect recipe for the perfect meal. She had spent the last few years cooking elaborate meals for the nuns as she tried out various options, but still hadn't found that one dish that made her nod her head with satisfaction. She scribbled away her findings in tiny notebooks that were often found all over the kitchen—under cookbooks, stuffed between spice jars or balanced precariously on top of a pile of lemons.

'Maybe I could grow some cinnamon,' suggested Sister Parsnip. 'Is cinnamon something you can grow?'

'I don't really think it's a plant,' said Sister Ruth doubtfully. She was already planning the next meal in her head. There was a ripe melon in the pantry that needed using up and she was sure she had a nice bit of dried ham somewhere for a sandwich.

'I'm sure I could still grow it,' Sister Parsnip insisted. She was often found in the vegetable gardens, her grey wimple twisted into a knot as she dug into the earth, trying to coax her plants into growing bigger and better. She was very sensitive about her hobby, and often took it very personally if no one wanted one of her beloved cabbages for dinner. 'I think I will definitely try to grow some,' she continued. 'We really should be eating more fresh vegetables.'

'I don't think cinnamon is a vegetable,' Sister Ruth started. 'It's more like a—'

'We should have an evening celebrating ancient hymns,' Sister Mildew interrupted, raising a frail finger. 'That's something we haven't had in a while.'

The other nuns groaned. At the ripe old age of eighty-two, Sister Mildew was the longest serving nun at the abbey and had a deep love of mid-century Latin choruses. This was a love that the other nuns did not share.

'We just had one of those,' Sister Agnes said quickly, exchanging glances with the other nuns. 'I'm sure we did. Didn't we just have one last week?'

'We haven't had a good old-fashioned evening of song for quite a while now, I don't think,' insisted Sister Mildew. 'I don't remember singing my special songs for you at all this year.'

Sister Ruth came around quickly with a bowl of dessert. 'Here you go, Sister Mildew,' she said. 'I know how much you love strawberries.' Sister Mildew grabbed her spoon and dug in happily, all thoughts of hymns temporarily discarded. With the older nun successfully distracted, the others settled down to enjoy their fruit. Well, most of them did, anyway.

'What I want to know,' said Sister Parsnip, who had been silently nursing her hurt feelings over her bowl of crumble, 'is what will happen to my lovely radishes if no one will let me put them in a stew? I planted so many of them and now no one wants to eat any.'

'I think I can use them for my next project,' said Sister Sparkplug, her eyes magnified behind an enormous pair of motorcycle glasses. She was an amateur inventor and was convinced that the glasses improved her ability to concentrate. 'I could possibly use them to create some sort of battery.' She sat back, her brow furrowed in concentration.

'Absolutely not!' Sister Parsnip said indignantly. 'These are good radishes. They're made for eating, not for destroying in one of your hare-brained inventions.' She shook her head fiercely. 'Not my radishes.'

'There's nothing wrong with my inventions!' Sister Sparkplug exclaimed. 'Some of them have made life better for all of us.' She pointed at a small tube-shaped machine with a butter knife attached to it that sat by the toaster. 'I don't know about you, but the Automatic Butterer makes my mornings easier and breakfast time is now a lot less complicated.'

'It takes ten minutes to butter one slice of bread,' Sister Ruth said, rolling her eyes. 'That's not really helping anyone.'

'You're missing the point!' Sister Sparkplug said hotly, leaning forward. 'It's doing something for you, so you can use that time to get something else done!' Tendrils of wiry brown hair started to escape out of her wimple as she spoke.

'Well, I'm still not letting you waste my radishes on that nonsense,' Sister Parsnip said, folding her arms stubbornly. 'They're absolutely wonderful this year.'

'In France, we eat the radish with some butter,' Sister Pauline said dreamily. 'But your radish here is very different. It is the taste.' She shrugged, rearranging her used cutlery neatly on her plate. 'The taste of everything is different here,' she summed up with a sigh. Although she now called the abbey her home, Sister Pauline occasionally found herself homesick for her country and often slipped into her native French when she found herself too agitated or excited to speak English.

'I'm sure I can think of a nice recipe for the radishes,' Sister Ruth said. 'They'll get used, don't you worry.'

'All that recipe nonsense,' Sister Beatrice cut in. 'You should stop all that and we should be eating vegetables the way the good Lord intended us to—raw.' Sister Beatrice never missed an opportunity to be contrary. Sent to Pistachio after spending ten years in a convent where the nuns hardly ever smiled, the others often felt that Sister Beatrice had been sent to the abbey to teach them to be patient and control their tempers.

'Ugh,' said Sister Ruth. 'No, not raw. I was reading one of the old food magazines in the attic, and I think I can make a lovely pasta dish with some shrimp—'

'We don't have any shrimp, though, do we?' Sister Beatrice cut in. 'We live on top of a mountain. There's no shrimp around anywhere here.'

'The pond behind the abbey might have an occasional tadpole at the very most,' agreed Sister Agnes. 'I have no idea where we'd get any shrimp.'

'We could always go down into the town and buy some provisions,' Sister Ruth suggested unconvincingly. 'I'm sure they have some nice seafood there, they're not too far from the coast.'

'Are you volunteering?' Sister Sparkplug leaned forward eagerly. 'If you are, I have a list of things I need so I can fix Vroom up a little. He's been having a few problems dealing with simple commands.' She smiled affectionately at her robot broom, who was trying unsuccessfully to sweep up a ball of fluff from the corner of the room. Sister Sparkplug had painstakingly built him from various scraps in her workshop, and although Vroom was always eager to help, he never quite managed to get things right.

'*I'm* not going out there,' said Sister Ruth, pouring more cream onto her crumble and making herself comfortable in her chair. 'You go and buy your own precious bits of stupid old machinery.'

'It's the Summer Festival today,' said the Reverend Mother hurriedly, trying to deflect the next argument. 'We received an invitation a few weeks ago. Apparently this year's event is meant to be their biggest and best one yet.'

'They say that every year,' Sister Beatrice looked unimpressed. 'All it means is that they improve themselves slightly each time.'

'I'm sure it's not safe down there,' said Sister Agnes, shuddering slightly. 'There's just so much crime everywhere and so much noise, too.'

'They certainly keep us awake during their festivals,' the Reverend Mother agreed. 'There was quite a lot of music from the valley last year. Didn't we have to soundproof the doors and windows with all the winter blankets?'

'I felt like a squirrel in a hole,' Sister Agnes said. 'It's the same every year. Most unpleasant.'

'Such a violent world out there,' Sister Beatrice shook her head dramatically. 'So much noise and music and dancing—leads to nothing but crime.'

'I think it's rather nice of them to invite us every year,' Sister Sparkplug said, scraping up the last bit of strawberry crumble from her bowl and wiping her mouth with her sleeve. 'It's nice and neighbourly.'

'Well, I'm sure they have good intentions,' the Reverend Mother sighed. 'They just don't understand how dangerous things can get when you aren't careful. One minute it's a friendly town festival, but before you know it, terrible things happen.' She paused and cocked her head to one side. 'Who put the blankets up to block the sound this year?' she asked. 'I just realized that I can't hear anything at all.' The nuns looked at each other, puzzled.

'I don't think we have them up,' Sister Parsnip said finally.

The Reverend Mother looked disbelievingly at them. 'Are you sure? It's never this quiet during the festival weekend.' The nuns shook their heads, one by one. 'That's very odd.' The Reverend Mother looked perplexed.

'Maybe you have the date wrong,' Sister Ruth said, getting up to collect the empty bowls from around the table. 'Maybe it's next weekend.'

'Speaking of the weekend,' Sister Parsnip said, 'I have a harvest of sweet potatoes due then. I hope you like them better than my poor radishes.'

Leaving the friendly chatter of the other nuns behind her, the Reverend Mother got up to go outside with Sister Agnes for their customary evening stroll in the garden. As she stepped out of the dining room, the Reverend Mother began to feel the first prick of uncertainty. Something didn't feel right—she could feel it in her toes. The two nuns walked to the front door, their footsteps echoing loudly as they walked down the dimly lit hallway.

'Do you think there's something wrong with our windows?' asked Sister Agnes, more than a little worried. 'Has the cold clogged them up in some way? Will we have to get someone from outside to come and fix them?' Sister Agnes believed that domestic repairs were only an excuse for strange people to come and scope out the abbey before planning a robbery. She slept with her two most prized possessions—her great-grandmother's Bible and a small silver hand mirror inlaid with mother-of-pearl—under her pillow at all times.

'I'm sure there's nothing wrong with the windows,' the Reverend Mother said, as she rummaged through the pockets in her habit for the keys to the door. 'I could hear Sister Ruth and Sister Parsnip arguing in the garden this afternoon when I was in my office, so they aren't suddenly soundproof.' She handed the keys to Sister Agnes. 'I'll be back in a minute,' she said, striding back down the hallway. 'I left the invitation in my office.'

Sister Agnes carefully unlocked the door and stepped out into the garden. The crisp evening air caught her by surprise and she rubbed her hands together to keep herself warm. Heading over to the furthest point of the garden, she looked down at the town of Pistachio, its twinkling lights dotted against the dark green of the valley. 'Everything still looks fine down there,' she said, as she heard the Reverend Mother join her outside. 'I think we just got the date wrong.'

The Reverend Mother pushed her reading glasses up her nose and pulled the Summer Festival invitation out of its envelope. She flipped it over, frowning. 'No, it definitely starts today,' she said. 'That's what it says here.' She put the card in her pocket and took her glasses off thoughtfully.

'I'm sure everything is just fine,' Sister Agnes said. 'Maybe they're just behaving themselves this year.'

The Reverend Mother didn't reply. She'd grown up in a small town herself and one thing she knew about people was that they never really behaved themselves. Especially on a day that involved pies and fireworks. 'Fireworks!' she said suddenly. 'It's almost time for the fireworks.'

The nuns stood at the edge of the garden together, looking out into the distance and waiting for the usual sounds to unfold. Previous years' celebrations had always ended with a riot of colours in the skies as the fireworks display went on until late in the night, combined with loud cheers that carried up the mountainside.

The Reverend Mother and Sister Agnes waited for a long time, but nothing happened. Apart from the sounds of the crickets just starting up their evening chirping and the occasional bird, the night stayed quiet.

'Something is not quite right,' said the Reverend Mother finally, and this time Sister Agnes agreed with her.

***

The next weekend, the nuns gathered by the windows again in case the festival had been postponed, but there were no sounds from the town. They put it down to a mistake on the invitation that was sent to them, and decided to wait another week. It was the same the weekend after that, however, and the one after that. Finally, even Sister Agnes had to agree that there were going to be no fireworks in Pistachio any time soon. The blankets were packed up and put back into the attic and Sister Ruth made a delicious orange drizzle cake that made most of them forget about the mysterious absence of the festival celebrations.

The Reverend Mother, however, couldn't shake off a feeling of unease. 'Do you think there's something strange going on in Pistachio?' she said to Sister Agnes one evening as they hung fresh laundry out to dry. 'Do you think we should check to see if everything's fine?'

'If there's something strange happening in the town, should we really be anywhere near it?' Sister Agnes asked doubtfully. She certainly wasn't keen on walking into the wide-open mouth of whatever troublesome mess the town had gotten itself into.

'We did agree to take care of the town,' the Reverend Mother said quietly, straightening out a striped pillowcase on the clothesline and clipping it in place. 'Back when the other nuns were here. We're meant to make sure the town stays protected.'

'They're fine down there,' Sister Agnes said, a little too brightly. 'I'm sure there's nothing wrong. Things were different when the old nuns were here. There hasn't ever been anything anything wrong with the town since I moved to this abbey.'

The Reverend Mother stood between the flapping sheets with her mouth full of wooden clothes pegs, trying to decide what to do. In all her time as head of the abbey, the hardest decision she'd ever had to make before this was what colour to paint the kitchen. 'I'm going to pray for guidance,' she announced, depositing the pegs with

Sister Agnes and heading towards the chapel. 'I like it better when someone else tells me what to do.'

On her way back through the garden, the Reverend Mother stopped at the pigeon loft to check for mail, stepping carefully to avoid droppings. Even though the abbey had a perfectly serviceable letterbox at the foot of the mountain, the nuns preferred to use pigeons because they considered them more reliable.

One of the letters was from the Most Reverend Mother up north, the head of the Order of the Assassin Nuns and the person responsible for sending them to the abbey. It was nothing important, just a general circular reminding them to always keep things running smoothly and report any problems or difficulties they were facing. The Reverend Mother stared at the piece of paper for a long time, and then decided what she was going to do. Maybe another addition to the abbey—a sensible, level-headed nun—would be just what they needed. Sister Pauline and Sister Sparkplug were young and inexperienced, Sister Mildew was too old to make much sense, and the others tended to mostly argue among themselves. Another senior nun at the abbey would help immensely, she decided. Someone she could share her concerns with and someone who would have logical explanations for things that made her feel uneasy. Things like the lack of fireworks at the festival down in Pistachio.

The Reverend Mother wrote out a quick note and filled in a form for a new member. Heading out to the loft again, she woke a sleepy pigeon and tied the message to its leg. 'Go on now, go drop this off,' she said, stroking the bird on its head. The Reverend Mother watched the bird disappear over the trees and headed back indoors, her mind at rest. Everything would be fine, she told herself. Someone was coming to help out at the abbey.

Help was certainly coming, but not quite in the form she expected.

3

A few weeks after the Reverend Mother sent a pigeon out for help and as the Assassin Nuns of Pistachio eagerly awaited their newest member, eleven-year-old Ann was being packed up and sent on her way from yet another abbey. Small, scrawny and overly freckled, with a head of unruly curls tied back with a piece of ribbon, Ann waved goodbye to the nuns from the Parish of Blessed Apples as she stepped through their wrought-iron gates for the last time, wondering what the next abbey would be like.

Wrapped in a blanket and left on the steps of a church when she was just a baby, Ann had grown up being passed from one set of nuns to another, playing in various choir stands and learning how to spell from hymn books. Now, with her patchwork suitcase in one hand and a rucksack slung across her shoulders, she had moved through more abbeys than she could count on both hands.

'Any idea who these Pistachio nuns are?' she asked Sister Felicity, who had been tasked with accompanying her to the bus stop.

'They're a small order,' said Sister Felicity, trying to pick up their pace. She had strict instructions to put Ann on the bus without any incident. With Ann, that was usually asking for a lot. 'I think that's one of the abbeys belonging to the Order of the Assassin Nuns,' she added, struggling with one of Ann's bags. 'How many books do you have in here, Ann? It's awfully heavy.'

'The Order of the Assassin Nuns?' Ann's eyes widened. 'Really? That's wonderful!'

Sister Felicity looked doubtful but didn't say anything. From the little she'd heard about the Assassin Nuns, she wasn't quite sure whether they were properly equipped to deal with someone like Ann. But then again, not many people were. 'Yes,' she said finally. 'I'm sure you'll enjoy the change, anyway. It's a little abbey on a mountaintop near a very small town.'

'Do you think they'll have a bookshop in the town?' Ann asked, brushing her hair out of her eyes. 'Or a library? Either would be fine.'

'I'm sure they do,' Sister Felicity said, pausing to catch her breath. 'You have plenty of books in any case. This bag feels like a sack of bricks.'

'Yes, they probably will have a library,' Ann agreed. 'I mean, who doesn't like books?' She dropped her bag down at the bus stop and turned to Sister Felicity. 'And they really wanted me?'

'That's what I was told,' Sister Felicity replied. 'Orders came from straight up, too. We had a letter from their Most Reverend Mother up north.' Her voice dropped into hushed tones. 'Apparently the Assassin Nuns wanted someone to train and she thought you'd be perfect.' She smiled at Ann fondly. Even though Ann had once trampled through her prize cabbage patch trying to catch a butterfly, Sister Felicity had quite a soft spot for her. She breathed a sigh of relief as the bus turned in around the corner. 'That's your ride,' she said to Ann, giving her a quick hug and handing her a ticket. 'Don't forget to wait for them at the bottom of the mountain; someone's coming to pick you up from there.' She paused for a minute and looked down at the little girl who once sent the Mother Superior to an emergency room by accidentally dropping a ladder on her while trying to help her pick apples. 'And please, do *try* to stay out of trouble,' she said firmly.

Ann climbed into the bus, turning around to wave at Sister Felicity again. The driver nodded at her as she pressed her ticket up against the glass partition that separated them, and soon they were on their way.

The bus was mostly empty and Ann picked a spot next to the window, sliding her suitcase under the seat with a practised ease that came from many, many bus rides to new homes. Sitting down, Ann did what she usually did while travelling—she stuck her head down to have a quick look under all the seats for any treasures that might have been accidentally left behind. She quickly found what she was looking for—an abandoned book below an empty seat—and fastened her seat belt only after it had been safely rescued and placed in her bag.

Ann watched the countryside as it raced past her window in a long, wavy green line, occasionally dotted with white flecks of sheep. As the journey continued, she noticed that the towns started to get smaller and the stretches between the villages got larger.

'Where are you off to today all on your own, dearie?'

Ann craned her neck up over the seats and saw an old woman wearing a blue straw hat smiling at her from two rows ahead. 'Hello,' she said cheerily. 'I'm off to Pistachio. Have you ever been there?'

'Pistachio?' the old woman repeated slowly. 'No, can't say that I've ever heard of it.' The bus hit a bump in the road and the old lady grabbed at her hat to keep it in place.

'I think it's quite small,' Ann said. 'But it's the home of some of the world-famous Assassin Nuns.'

'Haven't heard of them either, I'm afraid,' the woman said, adjusting her hat. 'It's most shocking. I really must start reading up on current affairs.'

'I've heard all these stories about the Assassin Nuns,' said Ann dreamily. 'They're like superheroes. A group of them once saved a family from a tiger.'

'Oh my, that does sound exciting,' the old woman said, in a tone that clearly implied that she thought Ann was making the whole thing up. She returned to staring out of the window, leaving Ann to happily do the same.

Ann was just about to fall asleep when the bus lurched and came to a stop by the side of a large field. The driver honked twice and gestured at Ann. 'Pistachio,' he called. 'This is your stop.'

Ann stared out of the window, confused. There was nothing outside, just a long expanse of what looked like a cornfield without a house in sight. 'Are you sure?' she asked. 'It doesn't really look like a town to me.'

'Pistachio,' the driver repeated, pointing at a sign on the road that claimed the town was right there. 'Hurry up, child. I've got six more hours of driving this thing before I can go home.'

Ann grabbed her bags and stepped off the bus. As she watched it rattle away, she felt a sense of growing dread. A quick sweep of her surroundings still revealed no sign of a town, just fields and a mountain in the distance. 'Oh, the mountain!' she said to herself suddenly, remembering the final set of instructions Sister Felicity had given her.

She picked up her bags again and headed over to the cluster of trees at the foot of the mountain, rehearsing what she'd say to the Assassin Nuns when she finally met them. She wished she'd learned how to ride a horse or speak a foreign language, as she was certain that their adventures would require a great deal of travel. Why else would they live in the middle of nowhere, she reasoned. It was clearly so they could use it as their base for secret operations.

Ann arrived at the path heading up the mountain and waited, as instructed. Keeping an eye out for a nun she was now certain would come dressed in a suit of armour, ten minutes went by before she actually noticed Sister

Agnes standing further up the road, wrapped in a long coat and leaning against a walking stick.

Sister Agnes didn't notice Ann either, mostly because she was expecting an older, scholarly nun and also because being so far away from the abbey made her nervous and distracted. She pulled the hood of her coat down, worrying about the possibly polluted air that was filling her lungs and wondering what Sister Ruth was making for the celebratory meal to welcome the new arrival.

Ann, meanwhile, was beginning to get impatient. Catching sight of what she thought was a shepherd waiting for missing sheep, she headed towards the figure to ask for directions to the abbey. 'Hello there!' she said loudly, causing Sister Agnes to jump. 'I was wondering if you could help me out. Do you know where the abbey is? I'm here to see the Assassin Nuns.'

Sister Agnes blinked, confused. She was looking at a child. A small, curly-haired child with two very large bags. Not an experienced senior nun. A child. 'The abbey?' she repeated falteringly.

'Yes, I'm going to live with the Assassin Nuns,' Ann said proudly. 'Have you heard of them?'

'I'm sorry, who are you?' Sister Agnes asked, scratching her head.

'I've been sent to live at the abbey,' Ann explained. 'They asked for me.'

'Oh,' Sister Agnes said faintly. She had a vague feeling that she was having a bad dream. 'Did you get off the bus here just now? The evening bus?'

Ann nodded impatiently. Her bags were starting to feel quite heavy and she couldn't understand why this odd stranger wouldn't give her directions.

'Did anyone else on the bus get off?' Sister Agnes persisted. 'An older nun, perhaps?'

'No,' Ann replied, shaking her head. 'Just me.'

Sister Agnes stared at Ann, considering the possibilities. Either this was some sort of misunderstanding, or the senior nun was really much younger than they'd expected. 'The Most Reverend Mother sent you here?' she asked again. 'They definitely told you to come to this abbey?'

Ann nodded. 'Can you please tell me where they live? Someone was supposed to meet me, but I think they forgot.'

'I'm from the abbey,' Sister Agnes said. 'I'm Sister Agnes and I'm here to pick up our new arrival.'

Ann raised her eyebrows. 'You're one of the Assassin Nuns?' she asked incredulously. 'I thought you were waiting for sheep.'

'Yes, I'm one of them,' Sister Agnes replied. 'You're . . . you're quite different from what I expected.'

'I'm so pleased to meet you!' Ann exclaimed, dropping her bags and reaching to shake sister Agnes' hand. 'Don't worry, I can run really fast and I'm a lot stronger than I look. I'd definitely be able to help with all your missions.'

Sister Agnes looked confused, but brushed it aside. 'This way, the abbey's just up this road here.'

'I'm so excited to be here,' Ann said as she followed Sister Agnes up the mountain, each of them carrying a bag. 'You don't happen to have any tigers around here, do you?'

'Tigers? Where?' Sister Agnes sounded startled.

They stopped for a breather halfway up the path, which was when Ann noticed the town around the other side of the mountain, tucked away and almost inaccessible by a regular road. 'Do you go down to the town often?' Ann asked. 'It does look lovely from here.'

'Oh no,' Sister Agnes replied. 'This is as far as we go, and only when there's someone to pick up. Terrible things happen out there.' She gestured vaguely at the great unknown.

'Really?' Ann asked with great interest. 'Will we have to intervene?'

'Oh dear, I really hope not,' Sister Agnes said, much to Ann's bewilderment.

They continued up the road in silence, each of them trying to make sense of the other. Sister Agnes, in particular, was having a hard time. 'You're absolutely sure there wasn't another nun on the bus?' she asked Ann again.

'I'm very sure,' Ann replied, grimacing as she carried her suitcase up the twisting mountain path. 'I've been living in abbeys for so long that I can now spot a nun from across a room. Sister Greta used to call it my nun-radar.' She scratched her head. 'I didn't notice you, though,' she said thoughtfully. 'Maybe my radar's gone rusty.'

'Who's Sister Greta?' Sister Mildew asked curiously.

'One of the nuns from the Order of Sacred Pastures,' Ann said. 'I lived there for four months a few years ago. They used to make some lovely cheese.'

'Ah, we do like a good cheese at the abbey,' Sister Agnes smiled. 'And there's the abbey right over there,' she said, pointing at a large stone building ahead of them.

'It's absolutely lovely,' said Ann, and she meant it. In the evening light, the abbey looked like something out of a book, surrounded by the strangest forest she'd ever seen. 'Are those trees completely green?' she asked, as they passed through the clearing that led to the front gate. 'Even the bark?'

Sister Agnes nodded proudly. 'That's the special forest we have here,' she said. 'Nothing quite like it anywhere else, they say.'

Ann walked down the path and stood outside the door for a minute, admiring her new home and already planning to go exploring as soon as she'd put her things away. The curtains were drawn and the lamps were on inside, giving the place a warm, homey glow, and the most delicious smell wafted through the windows.

'Right, I know I've got my keys somewhere,' Sister Agnes said, rummaging through her coat pockets. 'Ah, there they are.' Then, in a gesture that would soon change the lives of everyone in the abbey and in the town of Pistachio, Sister Agnes motioned at Ann to follow her through the doors and into the abbey.

4

Ann's first impression of the abbey was that there were an awful lot of pictures of old people everywhere. The lobby that she stepped into was painted a pale cream, but there were cracks on the wall where the plaster had come off, making it seem a bit like the subjects of the paintings were constantly being struck by lightning. There were two long tartan couches facing each other, with a round, glass-topped table in between, where a solitary banana of doubtful age sat in a wooden bowl.

Sister Agnes motioned Ann towards the couches as she attempted to fasten each of the front door's eleven bolts. The action was lost on Ann, who immediately wandered off in the opposite direction through the hallway that led to the rest of the house. After sliding the last lock into place and wondering how best to explain to Ann that all this had been a mistake, Sister Agnes took a deep breath and turned around, only to find herself faced with an empty room and a missing child.

Ann, in the meantime, was making her way down the short passage to the nuns' living quarters, the wooden floorboards creaking under her shoes. The walls were lined with more pictures, but these were all rather spectacular watercolours chronicling the exploits of a group of nuns. Picture after picture of them fighting an array of what appeared to be brightly dressed villains. Ann found herself quite fascinated by a particularly lurid one of the nuns battling what looked like a giant purple monster.

There was a door at the end of the passage with a handwritten sign over it that read 'Clean shoes only. Please!' Ann took a quick look at her feet and decided that her grubby boots wouldn't pass muster. Anxious to make a good first impression on the Assassin Nuns she was sure she would soon be going on adventures with, Ann took her shoes off and gently pulled the door open.

Peering through the doorway, Ann could see seven nuns seated around a dinner table, their plates piled high with food. There were two empty chairs at one end, presumably for Sister Agnes and herself. As Ann stared at them, fascinated, she had to admit these were the least ninja-like nuns she could have ever imagined.

At the head of the table sat a tall, thin woman, clad in a darker grey than the other nuns. She had a gleaming rosary around her neck and was eating her chicken pot pie with an air of quiet authority. Beside her, stabbing at her plate with much relish and no quiet authority whatsoever, sat a middle-aged nun with a pair of old-fashioned motorcycle goggles perched over a mass of wispy hair escaping from under her wimple. Further up, a nun with a copious amount of dirt on her clothes was deep in conversation with a tiny, wrinkled old woman who wore very round reading glasses, while a small, almost perfectly round nun in a flowered apron waved a ladle about excitedly at them. And right in front of Ann, two other nuns were arguing about something, one gesturing animatedly while the other shook her head, a frown stretched across her dour face.

Someone passed a steaming bowl of potatoes across the table and Ann felt her stomach start to grumble. Opening the door a bit wider, she stepped in and gave a polite cough.

'Intruder!' one of the nuns exclaimed loudly, pointing at Ann. There was a sudden cacophony of sound as cutlery clattered onto plates and chairs were pushed back. Ann found herself facing seven terrified faces.

'Hello?' she said falteringly, smiling at them in what she hoped was her most winning manner. The nuns, however, were frozen into place at the sight of the tiny trespasser in her striped socks. The Reverend Mother started to speak, but decided against it.

'There she is! I thought I'd lost her,' Sister Agnes said as she came bustling in and stood next to Ann, not quite sure what to do next.

'You lost a child?' asked Sister Parsnip, who was the first to regain the ability to speak.

'That child has no shoes,' Sister Ruth pointed out helpfully from across the table.

Sister Mildew continued to peer at Ann through her moon-shaped glasses. 'Is that an elf?' she asked curiously. 'It's very short.'

The Reverend Mother cleared her throat in an attempt to restore order. 'Sister Agnes,' she said. 'Who is this child and where is our esteemed guest?'

'Ah,' said Sister Agnes. 'Yes, the senior nun.' She paused to look intently at her own shoes. 'The bus . . .' Her voiced trailed away.

'How did you lose a child?' persisted Sister Parsnip. 'I don't understand. How on earth did you have a child to lose in the first place?'

Ann had, by this point, realized things weren't going to get very far unless she took matters into her own hands. 'My name is Ann,' she announced, stepping forward with a smile. The nuns immediately moved backwards in their chairs and a fork clattered to the floor.

'There was no other nun down there,' Sister Agnes explained quickly. 'Ann says she was sent here by the council. They told her where to get off the bus and everything.'

'You mean the council sent her to us?' Sister Ruth looked incredulous. 'Oh my word, that's definitely the youngest nun I've ever seen!'

'I'm not a nun,' Ann cut in. 'I've just always lived in abbeys from the time I was born. I stay in each one for a couple of months until it's time to move to the next.' She looked at the wary faces around the table. 'They told me this was my next one.'

As the nuns murmured among themselves, the Reverend Mother readjusted her glasses and walked over to Ann. 'Hello,' she said, reaching out for a handshake. 'I'm the Reverend Mother of this abbey.' She directed Ann to an empty chair at the table and sat down next to her. 'We're the Order of the Assassin Nuns,' she continued. 'It's just a small abbey and most of us have been here for around at least fifteen years now.'

'And we've never had a child here once in those fifteen years,' Sister Beatrice muttered. 'Not once.'

'Let me quickly introduce you to everyone,' the Reverend Mother said, gesturing at the nuns around the table, who were still staring at Ann with a mixture of fear and curiosity. 'Sister Ruth runs the kitchens, Sister Parsnip grows our wonderful vegetables, Sister Beatrice takes care of our birds and the lovely flowers outside, Sister Pauline looks after the laundry, Sister Sparkplug is in charge of repairs and maintenance, and Sister Agnes—who you've met—looks after filing and other such official matters.' The nuns nodded politely back at Ann.

'Hello,' Ann said again. 'It's very nice to meet all of you.' She put her bags down and took her rucksack off her back. 'I have a lot of books,' she explained, pointing at the luggage by her feet. 'I take them with me everywhere I go. It's like having friends you can carry around in a suitcase with you all the time, which is always handy.'

'Ah yes, of course,' said the Reverend Mother blankly.

'I'm very happy to be here,' Ann said. 'I've been wondering where my next abbey would be, and I never thought I'd be living with the wonderful Assassin Nuns!' She brushed a few errant strands of hair out of her eyes excitedly. 'I did like my old abbey, but I'm so much more excited about being here!'

'We're glad to have you, too,' the Reverend Mother said, exchanging a panicked glance with Sister Agnes. 'We're . . . excited as well.'

'But we've never had a child here before,' Sister Beatrice said grouchily. 'How are we going to take care of one?'

'I can take care of myself,' Ann said proudly. 'Sister Gloria from the Parish of Mute Swans always told me that I had a knack for surviving under the harshest conditions.' She smiled brightly at them. 'I think she said that because of the time I got stuck in the butter churn when I was a baby,' she added contemplatively. There was a crash as Sister Mildew's glasses slipped down her nose and landed in her plate. She blinked sleepily and looked around, confused.

'That's Sister Mildew,' the Reverend Mother said. 'She's in charge of the chapel and is very old.' The Reverend Mother leaned in towards Ann. 'Just don't say "hymn" in front of her and everything will be fine,' she whispered.

'Hymn!' Sister Mildew repeated, her ears perking up instantly as she heard her favourite word. 'Time for hymns!'

'No, Sister Mildew,' Sister Ruth said loudly, picking the glasses up from the plate and shaking a piece of broccoli off them. 'It's time for bed, not hymns. We'll sing some hymns tomorrow.' She placed the glasses back on Sister Mildew's nose.

'No,' Sister Mildew said stubbornly. 'It's always hymns tomorrow. I want to sing hymns now.' She folded her arms across her chest and pouted.

'All right,' Sister Beatrice said, exchanging a glance with the others. 'I'm going to look in on the chickens before we go to bed. Would you like to come with me, Sister Mildew? I know you like the little fluffy ones.'

'Fluffy little chickens!' Sister Mildew exclaimed happily, all thoughts of hymns forgotten.

'Sister Beatrice is right, we don't know what to do with a child,' said Sister Parsnip, looking at Ann critically. 'For instance, what do they eat? I'm sure I've read somewhere that you need to give them some sort of special food or they won't grow properly.'

'Don't be ridiculous,' said the Reverend Mother, waving her aside. 'Children are meant to have milk and dry bread before they go to bed. Everyone knows that.' Ann's eyes widened in alarm at the thought of all her evening meals being very much like prison food.

'We're all out of milk, though,' Sister Ruth looked concerned. 'I made us some custard for dessert and we're all out for tonight.'

'Oooh, custard,' Sister Agnes beamed, forgetting about Ann for a minute. 'I do like me some custard.'

'Do you think she could have some chicken pot pie instead?' Sister Ruth asked, looking at the leftovers on the table. 'I'm not sure if we have—'

'Oh yes, please!' Ann cut in hurriedly before any more terrible meal suggestions were made. 'Chicken pot pie is just fine.' Her eyes widened as Sister Ruth placed a generous slice with fried potatoes onto a plate and passed it over. 'That's lovely, thank you!' she exclaimed, digging in immediately. She'd almost forgotten how hungry she was.

The nuns watched in awe as Ann devoured her dinner. Her fork was a blur as mouthful after mouthful of crispy potato and chicken disappeared. 'Careful there,' Sister Sparkplug said. 'You don't want to injure yourself now.'

'We're not keeping her, are we?' Sister Ruth whispered to the Reverend Mother as she cleared the plates from the table. 'What on earth are we going to do with a child?'

'I did not know this was possible,' Sister Pauline said to them, her eyes still on Ann. 'A child who travels and lives in different abbeys. I have never seen such a thing before.'

'I'll send a pigeon out to the council tomorrow,' said the Reverend Mother quietly. 'I'm sure it's just a little muddle and we'll get it all sorted soon.'

'I do hope so,' Sister Parsnip spoke in hushed tones. 'A child in our abbey! I never thought I'd see the day.'

'If you can send her over after breakfast, Sister Ruth,' the Reverend Mother said, carrying an empty dish into the kitchen. 'I'll have a word with her and explain that we can't let her stay. I'm sure she'll understand—we're not really equipped to deal with children. She should be able to catch the afternoon bus from the foot of the mountain and go back to her last abbey.' The Reverend Mother returned to the dining room, where the nuns were still gathered around one side of the table watching Ann. 'I'm off to bed now,' she announced, stifling a yawn. 'I hope you have a comfortable night's sleep, Ann. There's a room upstairs made up for you.'

Ann nodded her head vigorously as she swallowed a large mouthful of chicken. 'Thank you,' she finally managed. 'Good night!'

'I still can't believe the council sent her to us,' said Sister Beatrice as the other nuns started to disperse. 'Next thing it'll be fairies coming in to roost on the trees outside.'

'Elves and fairies,' said Sister Mildew happily. 'It's Christmas again.'

***

After thoroughly demolishing her dinner, Ann was accompanied to her room by Sister Ruth, who helped her carry her bags up the winding stairs to the first floor. Having gotten over her initial nervousness with Ann, Sister Ruth had turned out to be a veritable chatterbox, intent on imparting as much information as she possibly could. 'And on Sunday, it's pancakes for breakfast,' she finished. 'After early morning prayers, of course. The promise of pancakes makes one much more thankful for everything.'

Ann opened the door to her new room and smiled as Sister Ruth flipped the light switch on. It was small and airy, with a colourful braided rug spread across the wooden floor. The walls were bare except for a small silver crucifix and a framed photograph of Albert Einstein. Next to the window was a bed with a small oak dresser next to it. A tartan blanket lay folded up on top of a wooden chest in the corner. There was a set of empty wooden shelves along one wall that Ann thought would make an excellent home for her collection of travelling books.

'Right, that's you all settled now,' said Sister Ruth, absently dusting the top of the dresser. 'I'll see you at breakfast tomorrow then, shall I? Do you have any questions?'

'Why Albert Einstein?' Ann asked curiously, pointing at the picture on the wall. She dropped her suitcase on her bed with a thump and opened it, spilling books and clothes over her duvet.

'Oh, this used to be Sister Sparkplug's old room,' Sister Ruth said. 'She fancies herself a bit of an inventor and likes her science. Always building these things that never really work properly.' She shook her head disapprovingly. 'You'll meet that frustrating robot broom soon enough.'

'A robot broom!' Ann exclaimed. 'You have a robot broom? That sounds like something out of a book.'

'She didn't follow the instructions in her book properly when she made that terrible thing,' Sister Ruth muttered. 'Anyway,' she said, yawning, 'I really should be off now. I'll shout out when it's time for breakfast tomorrow morning.'

'Do you normally go out on your adventures after breakfast?' asked Ann, putting a jumble of dresses into the wooden chest. 'Or is that more of an afternoon thing?'

'Our what?' Sister Ruth shot her a confused look.

'Adventures,' repeated Ann, grimacing as she tried to carry a pile of books taller than herself across the room.

'Ah,' said Sister Ruth inarticulately, as she headed for the door. 'Ah yes. The Reverend Mother will want a quick word with you tomorrow morning, I expect. She'll answer your questions. Goodnight!'

'Adventures,' she repeated to herself in disbelief, shaking her head as she walked out of the room.

5

Ann woke up the next morning to the sound of chickens. Or, more specifically, she woke up to the sound of chickens being chased by an exasperated nun clearly at the end of her tether. 'Out of my way, you silly things!' she heard someone shout as the angry squawks grew louder. 'It's like you WANT to be stepped on. Get out of my way!'

Ann sat up in bed and yawned as she took stock of her surroundings properly. The room wasn't the biggest one she'd ever had—she had spent a year living in the Sisters of Dewdrop Forest's conference room, which was the size of a small football field—but it certainly was a good-sized one. And now that most of her possessions were out of her suitcase and scattered around the room, it certainly felt more like home.

'Breakfast!' A voice called out from downstairs. 'Breakfast in ten minutes!'

Ann got out of bed and stretched her arms out. The braided rug on the floor felt knobbly under her bare feet, but it was a pleasant sensation. If she remembered the conversation with Sister Ruth correctly, there would be pancakes for breakfast today, and pancakes were always an excellent reason to get out of bed.

Heading towards the sink, she discovered that the nuns had left her a fresh tube of mint-flavoured Holy Toothpaste. 'Hurray!' she said to herself. None of the other nuns she had lived with ever let her use any of the Holy Provisions that were made specially for the abbeys. Ann had always wanted to use Holy Umbrellas, because she'd heard that they made the raindrops that rolled off them look multicoloured. She made a mental note to keep an eye out for them here.

The window over the sink looked out at a vegetable patch and as Ann cleaned her teeth vigorously with her new extra-foamy toothpaste, she counted twenty-three different plants, tomatoes being the only ones she could name. She made a mental note to look up the uses of plants in battle, as she was certain the nuns were growing some sort of horticultural weapons to help them in their missions.

A large, cloth-covered head suddenly popped up, blocking her view of the garden, as a nun bent down to pull a carrot out from the ground. Ann watched as Sister Parsnip made her way around the vegetable patch, the bottom of her habit trailing through the mud as she fussed over her plants and disposed of any errant weeds with swift ferocity. The favoured carrot was patted lovingly, and then placed carefully in a pocket in the recesses of her habit.

As Ann watched, Sister Parsnip smiled at each plant in her tidy garden, her gaze moving from one to the next until she reached Ann's cheerful face at the window, smiling broadly as she continued to brush her pearly whites. 'Hello!' mouthed Ann, before disappearing from view to wash her face. She reappeared a few seconds later, her smile still in place on a damp face. 'Hello, Sister Parsnip!'

Sister Parsnip, reeling slightly from the shock of seeing a tiny, foamy-mouthed child grinning at her through the window, tugged at her wimple to keep it from slipping off. 'Hello,' she said faintly. 'Lovely morning, isn't it?'

Ann pulled the sash on her window until it opened, and then stuck her head out for a better view. 'This is an amazing garden, Sister Parsnip,' she said, looking at the vegetable patch with great interest. 'How many things do you have growing here?'

Sister Parsnip beamed at her. 'Thank you!' she said. 'Not many people appreciate the work it takes to bring the food to their table.' She pointed at the neat rows in front of her. 'I have fourteen different kinds of vegetables here,' she said proudly. 'Some of them are very special varieties that you wouldn't normally find in this part of the world. There are also some fruit trees in the back garden.'

'Oh wow,' Ann said. 'Do you grow them all yourself?'

'I do indeed!' Sister Parsnip said warmly. 'It's hard work but there's no better feeling than having your first beautiful harvest.' She paused and cocked her head to one side. 'That's Sister Ruth calling us,' she said, lifting her muddy skirts up and stepping back on to the path. 'I'd best change quickly,' she explained. 'Sister Ruth tends to get upset when there's mud in her kitchen.'

Later, at the breakfast table, Ann discovered that she'd been right. A tall stack of pancakes sat in the middle of the table, with bright cereal bowls on either side. The nuns were already at the table and had left her a spot between Sister Sparkplug and Sister Parsnip, whose wimple was still askew.

Ann sat down and filled her bowl with a small portion of honey oats, making sure to leave plenty of room for pancakes, and stretched her arm out to reach for the milk. 'Let me help you with that,' Sister Sparkplug said, picking the jug up and pouring a generous splash into Ann's cereal. Her hand slipped as she was putting it back on the table, and a thin stream of milk trickled down and made a tiny puddle on the floor.

'Oh dear! I'm sorry about the spill, Sister Ruth,' said Sister Sparkplug apologetically. 'I'll get that cleaned up right away.' She pulled a whistle out of the folds of her habit and gave two sharp blasts. Vroom appeared at the door and made a beeline for the milk. 'Be a good chap and sort out the floor, would you?' Sister Sparkplug said, giving his motor a pat as he passed by her.

Vroom buzzed happily, then ejected a sponge from his base and proceeded to mop up the spill, squeaking constantly. Ann watched, captivated, as he then suddenly lost interest in the spill and moved forward, driving himself into the wall repeatedly.

'He's malfunctioning again,' said Sister Agnes, reaching for the butter knife with one hand and a blueberry muffin with the other.

'No, Vroom!' Sister Sparkplug called out, shaking her head. 'Stop that! The exit is the other way!'

'I didn't quite get him right the first time,' she explained to Ann, as they both watched him turn around in circles as he tried to find the door. 'I think he needs a proper redo and some new wiring, but I can't bring myself to take him apart now.'

'You made Vroom?' Ann eyes widened as she watched the little robot broom scurry across the floor.

'Yes, I did,' Sister Sparkplug said as she poured herself a glass of juice. 'He's a bit of a work in progress, though,' she added.

'Can I see some of your other inventions?' Ann asked, still wide-eyed. 'I've read a book about Thomas Edison, but I've never met a real-life inventor before.'

'Well, of course!' Sister Sparkplug said, very pleased at being compared to Thomas Edison, whose picture she had in her room, pinned next to a print of *The Last Supper*. 'I'm usually in my workshop until lunchtime, so come on by and have a nosy around.'

Sister Mildew lifted the milk jug with a shaky hand. 'I knew a Thomas once,' she began, as the jug wobbled precariously. 'He was a cat.'

'Let me help you with that, Sister Mildew,' Sister Agnes offered, taking the jug from her. 'Would you like some honey with your cereal?'

'Thomas was a good cat,' continued Sister Mildew dreamily, ignoring her. 'And now he's a rose bush in the back garden.' She picked up her bowl of cereal and drank the milk straight from the bowl.

'Seconds, anyone?' the Reverend Mother asked, spearing a pancake with her fork and passing the serving plate down the table. Ann helped herself to two pancakes and some fruit, accidentally knocking a blueberry out of the fruit bowl in the process. Suddenly, a tiny furry creature ran across the table and grabbed the blueberry. Ann's eyes widened as it proceeded to carefully sniff at the piece of fruit and then took a delicate bite.

'That's not Thomas the cat,' said Sister Mildew helpfully. 'Thomas was much bigger.'

'SISTER PAULINE,' thundered Sister Ruth, a frown creasing her normally cheerful face. 'Can you please get rid of that horrible creature?'

Sister Pauline, who was deep in conversation with the Reverend Mother, dropped her fork and scrambled around to Ann, muttering apologies. Picking up what Ann correctly identified as a guinea pig, she dropped him into her pocket, berating him in singsong French.

'I don't know what the abbeys are like in France,' Sister Ruth continued, 'but over here we keep our pets far away from the food on the table.'

'I'm sorry,' said Sister Pauline apologetically. 'The guinea pig, he does not like my pocket when there is fun happening outside.' She bent down to look at him. *'Vilain cochon d'Inde!'* she said to the little furry creature,

shaking her head at him. *'Combien de fois devrais-je te dire de ne pas t'enfuir?'*

'What did you say to him?' Ann whispered, fascinated by the little exchange.

'I explain that he must not do this again,' Sister Pauline whispered back at Ann. 'He is with me all the time so he does not speak the English.'

'I thought she was getting rid of that nasty thing,' said Sister Beatrice, wrinkling her nose. 'I have nightmares that it gets into my room and under the covers.' She shuddered as she shot a look at him, now safely swathed in Sister Pauline's habit.

'Oh, it's a friendly pet and has never hurt anyone,' said Sister Sparkplug, attacking her pancakes with gusto. 'Leave the little one alone.' A brown stain that looked suspiciously like motor oil stretched across the edge of the tablecloth where she was sitting, but Sister Ruth hadn't noticed it yet.

The Reverend Mother took a sip of orange juice and cleared her throat. 'Ann, can I please see you in my office after breakfast?' Sister Ruth and Sister Beatrice exchanged knowing glances. 'There are a few matters we need to discuss.'

'Oh yes,' Ann nodded, certain that this would be about the Assassin Nuns' exciting duties and how she would fit into the scheme of things. 'I'll come as soon as I've helped Sister Ruth with the tidying up.'

'That's fine,' the Reverend Mother said. 'It's just down the corridor and to the right.'

'Did you grow these tomatoes as well, Sister Parsnip?' Ann asked. She picked the last slice off the serving plate with her fingers and popped it into her mouth. 'They're really very nice.'

'Yes, I did,' Sister Parsnip said, a smile breaking across her face. 'Those are my lovely heirloom tomatoes. Planted them earlier this year and they've been nothing but a delight to me since.' She pushed her plate aside and leaned towards Ann as she broke into a whisper. 'I haven't told anyone, but I'm currently trying to grow Cherokee Purple tomatoes.'

'Are they really purple?' Ann whispered back. 'On the inside, I mean.'

'Properly purple,' replied Sister Parsnip, her eyes wide and excited. 'It's going to revolutionize the way we eat here!'

'Are you talking about your garden again?' Sister Beatrice rolled her eyes from across the table. 'If you're done with breakfast, let me remind you that it's your turn to polish the candlesticks in the chapel this week.'

'I can't wait to see the purple tomatoes,' Ann whispered to Sister Parsnip, as the nun dusted the crumbs off her lap and stood up. 'They sound very exciting!' Sister Parsnip nodded happily and was about to continue the conversation, when she caught Sister Beatrice's eye and left the room hurriedly instead.

'Where's the chapel?' Ann asked. 'Can I see it?' The nuns were starting to leave the table, and the Reverend Mother had already retired to her office.

'Maybe later,' Sister Agnes said. 'They need to finish tidying up in time for late afternoon prayers and Sister Parsnip is easily distracted. Besides, you have your meeting with the Reverend Mother.' She looked away awkwardly.

'I'll just put these away first,' Ann said, stacking the dirty plates into a pile and taking them through to the kitchen. 'Those were lovely pancakes, Sister Ruth,' Ann said as she passed her. 'They were the best I've ever had.'

'Even better than the ones they make at the Abbey of the Overly Red Bricks?' Sister Ruth paused on her way to the sink, turning around to look at Ann. 'Sister Gloria never fails to mention their immense popularity in the Christmas newsletter.'

'Much better,' said Ann, nodding her head firmly. 'I lived there for ten months and yours are much better.' Ann deposited the pile of dishes by the sink and wiped her hands down the sides of her dress as she returned to the dining room.

'Well, they're just pancakes,' Sister Ruth said nonchalantly as she began to do the dishes, but she couldn't keep the smile from her face as she scrubbed the last bit of batter off the mixing bowl. She'd always suspected that Sister Gloria was a bit of a bragger when it came to her culinary skills.

After putting the last dish away, Ann dusted the crumbs off the table and started to attack a few stubborn syrup stains with a damp cloth. Sister Pauline brought a vase of tulips in and put them down in the centre of the table. 'That is good,' she said approvingly as Ann wiped the last sticky stain off the table. 'Very clean now.'

'Can I meet the guinea pig?' Ann asked as she stared at the twitching nose that stuck out of the folds of Sister Pauline's habit as she moved.

'Yes, of course!' Sister Pauline beamed at the prospect of introducing her pet to an admirer. 'Come out, my precious.' She carefully lifted him out of her pocket and set him down on the palm of her hand.

Ann and the guinea pig stared at each other with wide, curious eyes. Ann reached out a tentative finger and stroked its head, earning her a wide smile from Sister Pauline. 'What's his name?' she asked, as he scampered down Sister Pauline's arm and then back up again, clearly fascinated by Ann's hair.

'Bonjour!' replied Sister Pauline. 'Good French name.'

'Hello, Bonjour,' Ann said, stroking the guinea pig again.

'No, no,' said Sister Pauline, shaking her head. 'Not Bonjour. His name is Bonjour!, you know, with the dash of excitement.' She smiled at him fondly. 'He is a very—how do you say it—expressive animal.' Bonjour! responded by lying on his back and stretching his tiny limbs out ecstatically as Ann rubbed his tummy.

'Ann!' Sister Beatrice appeared behind her. 'The Reverend Mother will see you now.' She wrinkled her nose again at the sight of Bonjour!. 'Please make sure you wash your hands before you go in there.' Bonjour!, sensing that he was being referred to with disrespect, responded by turning his back on Sister Beatrice and letting out a tiny sniff.

6

The Reverend Mother's office was a small, cramped room with four large and feathery potted plants framing a tiny wooden desk. Various pictures of nuns—some benevolent, some bored—were crammed on one wall, while a very big filing cabinet occupied the other. The carpet was a faded green, but Ann could barely see it, as the floor was covered with cardboard boxes spilling over with what looked like a lifetime's worth of unopened mail. The Reverend Mother sat behind the desk, a pair of glasses perched on her nose and a slightly uncomfortable expression on her face.

'Hello,' said Ann brightly, stepping over boxes as she made her way across the room.

'I'm afraid there's nothing to sit on,' the Reverend Mother said apologetically. 'No one ever comes to talk to me while I'm in here.' She pulled a small stepladder out from under her desk and leaned over her desk to hand it to Ann. 'This will have to do for now.'

Ann cleared some floor space, then perched on top of the stepladder and dangled her feet as she examined the pictures on the wall. 'Who's that?' she asked, pointing at a particularly severe-looking nun dressed in white.

'Sister Angelica,' replied the Reverend Mother. 'She was one of the earliest nuns here. She's the one who set up the back gardens and built the birdhouses. Delightful woman.'

'She doesn't look very delightful,' observed Ann, squinting at the picture. 'She looks terribly unhappy.'

'Oh no,' said the Reverend Mother, shaking her head. 'She was the most cheerful person around. She was just allergic to smiling.'

'No one's allergic to smiling!' Ann exclaimed. 'I'm pretty certain that's impossible.'

'Well, she really was,' said the Reverend Mother. 'They say she tried to smile at a kitten once, but had a terrible bout of flu immediately after.' Ann digested this piece of information as she continued to stare at the pictures while the Reverend Mother shuffled a few papers around on her desk, not quite sure how to begin.

There was a sharp knock on the door and Sister Ruth stuck her head in, somewhat out of breath. 'Hello,' she said, gasping slightly. 'Just checking in to see how everything is going.'

'Is everything alright?' the Reverend Mother asked.

'Everything's fine!' Sister Ruth replied. 'Just catching my breath for a second.' She clutched at the door frame with one hand as her breathing evened out. 'Running does that to me,' she added. 'Hello Ann, how's the meeting going?'

'Hello,' Ann said. 'The Reverend Mother was just going to start.'

'Oh, excellent.' Sister Ruth smiled. 'Excellent.' She opened the door wider and adjusted her wimple, smiling broadly at both of them.

'Can I help you with anything?' the Reverend Mother asked.

'Oh no,' replied Sister Ruth. 'I was just wondering if Ann could come help me in the kitchen afterwards. I have all this organizing that I need done.'

'Organizing?' the Reverend Mother looked confused.

'Oh yes,' said Sister Ruth. 'Spices and herbs and all my special recipes that need to be filed away neatly. Also many, many other such things.' She looked intently at the floor. 'All of that needs organizing before the summer. It'll take her weeks to finish.'

'Weeks,' repeated the Reverend Mother faintly.

'Maybe more,' said Sister Ruth solemnly. 'Months? Who knows?'

'I see,' the Reverend Mother said, looking very much as though she didn't.

'I'll expect you in the kitchen immediately after your meeting then, Ann,' Sister Ruth said, backing out of the doorway and closing it firmly behind her.

The Reverend Mother stared at the closed door, her mouth slightly ajar. In the many years she'd been at the abbey, she'd never known Sister Ruth to run anywhere, unless there was a possibility of food involved. 'Right,' she said finally, shaking her head slightly and turning back to face Ann. 'I think you know why we're here.' She smiled at the girl tentatively.

'Oh yes,' said Ann. 'I've heard about all your exploits. I'm happy to help in any way, but I should probably tell you that running and kicking are my two strengths.' She stretched a leg out to demonstrate, nearly knocking over a pile of envelopes.

'Running and kicking,' repeated the Reverend Mother, starting to fidget with her papers again.

'I think I'd be very good at carrying messages during your missions,' Ann continued earnestly.

'Ah,' said the Reverend Mother. 'Sister Agnes tells me you were asking her a few questions earlier about . . . our missions.'

'I've heard a lot about the Assassin Nuns,' Ann said. 'All the stories about how you uphold the peace and fight for good.'

'Oh yes,' said the Reverend Mother, the light dawning in her eyes. 'You're talking about the old Assassin Nuns.'

'You don't look that old to me,' Ann said kindly. 'There's just a little bit of grey in your hair, but not too much.'

'Not us,' said the Reverend Mother. 'The other ones, the nuns who lived here when I first came to the abbey.' She leaned forward, crossing her arms on the desk in front of her. 'They actually used to go out there all the time,' she whispered.

'Out there?' Ann looked puzzled. 'Like, into space?'

'Dear me, no,' the Reverend Mother said. 'I mean outside the gates. They used to actually leave the abbey on a regular basis.' She shook her head. 'So brave but so very foolish.'

'Do you not leave the abbey?' Ann asked.

'We haven't really left since the old nuns retired fifteen years ago,' replied the Reverend Mother. 'I saw what they had to deal with and it's much too dangerous out there for us.' She shook her head rapidly. 'No, we stay here where it's safe.'

'What's out there?' Ann's mind instantly jumped to various terrifying scenarios.

'People,' said the Reverend Mother gravely. 'Also, germs, rusty nails and burglars hiding in the dark.' She furrowed her brow as she tried to think. 'Road accidents, sharp objects, old chewing gum under tables, flooding rivers and rotten eggs.' She readjusted her glasses and suppressed a small shudder. 'And the common cold,' she added. 'It's a silent killer.'

'A cold!' Ann said incredulously. 'There's no reason to be afraid of a cold!'

'That's what eventually struck down poor Sister Angelica,' the Reverend Mother said, glancing at the picture on the wall. 'They say she caught the sniffles one day while picking berries for a pie and it was all downhill from there.'

Ann still looked unconvinced. 'Those aren't really things to be afraid of,' she said. 'It's not really that dangerous out there.'

'This is where we live now,' the Reverend Mother smiled placidly. 'It's safe here on top of the mountain and the ideal place to grow turnips.'

'No banishing evil or wrestling with tigers?' Ann asked unhappily.

'I'm afraid we're just a small, quiet abbey,' said the Reverend Mother. 'Which brings me to my original point.' She paused for a second, distracted by the hypnotic movement of Ann's striped socks as she swung her legs back and forth. 'I'm afraid that we're a very small group here and we just can't have another—'

The Reverend Mother was interrupted by a frantic knock on the door. 'Come in,' she said.

Sister Pauline entered the room with Bonjour!'s whiskered nose sticking out of her pocket. 'I just come for a social visit,' she said, refusing to meet the Reverend Mother's eye. 'How is everybody here?'

'We're fine,' said the Reverend Mother. 'We're just—'

'The meeting is going good? No problems?' Sister Pauline asked Ann anxiously. Bonjour! took the opportunity to emerge from her pocket and run down her arm to investigate the lovely piles of paper all around the room, but she grabbed him quickly and returned him to his hiding place in one hasty movement.

'Just starting,' Ann explained. 'The Reverend Mother was telling me about Sister Angelica and the other Assassin Nuns.'

'Good, good,' Sister Pauline said, pushing her glasses up her nose. 'I was wondering if Ann would want to have some lessons of French?' She shot a glance at the Reverend Mother. 'It is good to learn,' she continued. 'Knowing the European languages is very—how do you say it—enriching for the mind.'

'Oh,' said the Reverend Mother, at a slight loss for words. 'Yes, I suppose so.'

'Very good!' said Sister Pauline, waving her arms about. 'I will make a lesson plan now for you. We will start tomorrow morning after the breakfast.' She grabbed the guinea pig again, just as he was about to escape. *'Vilain cochon d'Inde, pas bien!'* she said to him, rubbing the top of his head. 'He needs some exercise,' she explained. 'I will take him for a walk in the garden now.'

'How do you take a guinea pig for a walk in the garden?' Ann asked after she left. 'I thought they usually just lived in cages and slept a lot.'

'I'm not completely sure,' said the Reverend Mother. 'Sister Sparkplug invented a miniature leash for him, but he usually just runs around in circles until Sister Pauline gets tangled up and needs assistance.' She sighed and adjusted her glasses. 'Now where were we?'

'You were telling me about how you are afraid of eggs,' Ann reminded her helpfully.

'Not eggs,' said the Reverend Mother, waving a hand at her. 'Eggs are wonderful, wonderful things. Sister Ruth makes a beautiful omelette with fresh peas and peppers with just a touch of rosemary.' Her eyes started to glaze over as she stared into the distance. 'Rotten eggs,' she said finally, shaking her head. 'That's what's dangerous. They say people out there just leave them around until they go so bad that they explode.'

'I've never heard of a rotten egg exploding,' said Ann. 'Not once.'

'I'm sure I've heard of many instances,' said the Reverend Mother vaguely. 'These things are always happening.'

'Do you really never leave the abbey?' Ann asked. 'Not even to go shopping?'

'We have everything we need here,' the Reverend Mother said proudly. 'We bake our own bread, grow our own vegetables, raise our own chickens and sew our own clothes.'

'What about the post?' asked Ann, looking at the numerous boxes of unopened mail spread out in front of her. 'Do you have a post office up here as well?'

'Oh no,' said the Reverend Mother. 'Don't be silly. We have carrier pigeons.'

'You send your mail through carrier pigeons?' Ann's eyes widened. 'Doesn't that take forever?'

'It does,' admitted the Reverend Mother. 'Most of the letters we eventually receive contain information that's too old to do anything with.' She sighed as she looked at the piles of mail on the floor. 'That's why I don't really bother opening most of them,' she added. 'I really need to give this place a good tidying up.'

'Is that why you weren't expecting me?' asked Ann. 'Everyone here seemed very surprised when I turned up. Have you not had the letter yet?'

'Ah yes, about your arrival,' said the Reverend Mother. 'That's why I asked you in here, you see.' She took a deep breath. 'We actually sent a request out for—'

There was a loud rap on the door again and a slightly dishevelled Sister Parsnip had already barged in by the time the Reverend Mother registered the knock. 'We're doing fine here,' the Reverend Mother said quickly, before Sister Parsnip could get a word out.

'The meeting's only just started,' added Ann, enjoying the unexpected interruptions that morning.

'Ah, splendid,' said Sister Parsnip happily. 'Anyone fancy an after-breakfast carrot?' She rummaged through the pockets of her habit and emerged with two carrots, still dusted with a fine layer of earth. 'Pulled them out myself just now, so they're nice and fresh.' She held them out enticingly. Both Ann and the Reverend Mother shook their heads in unison as they watched bits of the garden fall onto the carpet. 'I'll just save them for an afternoon snack then,' Sister Parsnip said, putting them back in her pocket.

'Is everything alright?' the Reverend Mother asked wearily.

'Just grand,' Sister Parsnip said. 'I just dropped in to ask whether Ann is any good with a trowel.'

'A trowel?' asked the Reverend Mother. 'Why a trowel?'

'Ann was admiring my vegetable patch earlier this morning,' Sister Parsnip explained. 'I thought she might like the opportunity to learn how to garden properly from a professional.' She brushed a few bits of dirt off her habit. 'I mean myself,' she clarified, leaning conspiringly towards Ann. 'I have a bit of a green thumb, if I may say so. Last year I had a harvest of some beautiful aubergines.' She smiled proudly at both of them.

'I've tried to garden a couple of times,' said Ann. 'But it's never really turned out very well. I don't think plants like my fingers very much.' She wrinkled her nose and looked down at her offending digits.

'Rubbish,' said Sister Parsnip briskly. 'We'll fix that right away. I have some weeding to do this evening that would be a perfect start, and I'm sure we can find you a pair of gloves and a spade somewhere.' She pulled a carrot out of her pocket again and vaguely brushed the side of it before taking a big crunchy bite. 'That's a lovely bit of veg,' she said to herself, chewing carefully. 'Just lovely. Time to go check on the tomatoes now, I think. Don't want them feeling left out.'

'This meeting isn't really going anywhere, is it?' observed Ann, as Sister Parsnip left the room, still muttering to herself. 'What did you want to tell me?'

'I suspect it doesn't really matter any more,' said the Reverend Mother, with the hint of a twinkle in her eye. 'You seem to have made quite an impression on all the nuns here already.'

'People always say that to me,' Ann said thoughtfully. 'Usually when it's time for me to move on to the next abbey.'

'That's not quite what—' the Reverend Mother started saying, before being interrupted by the now-familiar knock on her door.

'Hello there,' said Sister Sparkplug brightly, entering the room with Vroom in tow. 'How's every—'

'She's staying,' the Reverend Mother cut in, shaking her head in resignation. 'Ann's staying. Please tell the others that they don't have to keep barging in with offers to do things with her.'

'Top-notch!' Sister Sparkplug said, while Vroom buzzed in appreciation. 'I'll inform the rest now,' she added to the Reverend Mother as she was leaving the room. 'Sister Mildew was going to come in next and demand that Ann be taught some Latin hymns.'

'That's a relief,' the Reverend Mother said to herself, shuddering inwardly at the prospect of having to deal with the conveniently deaf Sister Mildew when she was upset about something.

'So what is it that you were going to say?' asked Ann. 'About my arrival at the abbey not being expected?'

'Nothing really,' the Reverend Mother replied, standing up and smiling warmly at Ann. 'Welcome to your new home.'

7

'What about school?' Sister Beatrice asked suddenly one afternoon as she sat reading a book about how to prevent blight in rose plants. 'The only school here is all the way down in Pistachio and it's far too dangerous to go there. What's the child going to do about school?'

The nuns were gathered in the living room listening to a record on the old player, while Ann was curled up on a cushion in front of the fire, playing with Bonjour!. She'd been at the abbey for over a week and was starting to get used to the nuns, although the nuns were taking longer to get used to her.

'Does she really need to go to school?' Sister Parsnip asked, scratching her head. 'Are you sure that's necessary? I don't really remember learning anything important there.'

'Nonsense,' said Sister Beatrice firmly. Ann was quickly learning that this was the nun's favourite word. 'Of course she has to go. The child needs to learn how to read and write.'

'I can read and write!' Ann said, sitting up indignantly. 'I've read over a hundred books!' Bonjour! scurried up her shoulder and straight into her fascinating hair—something he'd wanted to do from the day he first met this tiny human.

'You still do need to go to school,' the Reverend Mother said thoughtfully. 'I'm fairly certain there are rules about those things and we could get into quite a lot of trouble.' Bonjour! stuck his head out of Ann's brown curls and twitched his nose in agreement.

'I used to teach,' Sister Agnes said, her brow furrowed in concentration as she worked on a cross stitch sampler of rabbits holding large cupcakes. 'We had a school right next to my previous abbey.' She put her needle down carefully and stretched her legs out. 'I used to teach science and geography, and sometimes I'd help with algebra as well.' She smiled at Ann, who started to look decidedly green on hearing the word 'algebra'. 'I'd be happy to help out.'

'That's settled then,' the Reverend Mother said, sighing with relief. 'I'll send the pigeons out to a nearby abbey for some reading material this afternoon and Sister Agnes and Ann can start having lessons in the chapel every morning.'

'Lessons?' Sister Mildew perked up instantly. 'I give excellent lessons.' She stared at each of the nuns around the room. 'Who wants lessons?' she asked eagerly.

'It's lessons for school, Sister Mildew,' the Reverend Mother said loudly, leaning towards her. 'It's for Ann. She needs to go to school.'

'Latin is very important,' Sister Mildew said solemnly, wagging a bony finger at Ann. 'I will make sure the elf learns it well.'

'No, not you, Sister Mildew,' the Reverend Mother tried to explain. 'Sister Agnes used to be a teacher, so Ann will be taking lessons from her. They don't teach Latin in schools any more, so it's just the other regular subjects.' She leaned in a little closer. 'Ann is a child, not an elf,' she added, speaking directly into Sister Mildew's ear. 'She's just a little shorter than us because she hasn't finished growing yet.'

'That's rubbish,' Sister Mildew said, shaking her head furiously. 'She's too short to be a regular person.' The Reverend Mother sat back in her chair, giving up. 'I will teach her all the Latin I know,' Sister Mildew continued. 'And one day, she may be good enough to sing hymns with me.'

Ann's eyes widened, but Sister Pauline shook her head reassuringly. 'Don't worry,' she whispered. 'The old one, she will forget. She forgets everything.' She picked Bonjour! up carefully from Ann's shoulder and put him back into her pocket, stroking his fur. *'Reviens ici, petit chenapan!'* she said to him fondly. 'You are excited about your lessons, yes?' she asked, turning to Ann.

'I don't like lessons very much,' Ann said truthfully. 'People are always making me read things I don't want to and everything they teach me seems very useless.'

'I suppose they think those things will come in handy someday,' Sister Parsnip said, absently fidgeting with a radish. 'My school used to place far too much importance on silly things like calculating the number of sweets in a barrel when it would have been so much handier to learn the names of common garden plants.'

'They don't teach common sense in schools at all,' Sister Beatrice agreed. 'No one seems to care about whether children have basic skills at all. It's just this fancy maths and languages no one ever uses any more.' She shot an exasperated look at Sister Mildew as she spoke.

'No one taught me how to build,' Sister Sparkplug said. 'I wish I'd had classes on how to wire machinery properly instead. Would have stopped me from giving myself more than a few nasty electric shocks!'

'No one taught me how to cook either,' Sister Ruth said. 'I learned by making lots of mistakes and ruining a depressing number of apple pies.' She put her book aside and took her reading glasses off, yawning. 'I'm going to make dinner now,' she said to Ann, standing up and stretching her limbs out. 'Would you like to come help me?'

***

Ann decided that the kitchen was her favourite place in the abbey. Rows of gleaming dishes sat on the sturdy wooden shelves that ran across the walls and strings of garlic and dried herbs hung from the rafters, adding a whiff of the exotic to the room. The steady hum of the large white refrigerator in the corner, combined with the gentle ticking of the clock above the sink, was both soothing and pleasant.

Sister Ruth and Ann sat at the table shelling peas, while Sister Ruth kept a watchful eye on her soufflé in the oven. 'Most people are afraid of soufflés,' she told Ann, rhythmically splitting the pods open and dropping the fresh peas into a bowl before moving on to the next. 'They think it's hard to get it just right. They're wrong.' She paused and popped a pea into her mouth. 'The trick is to make sure your eggs are at room temperature before you start. Take them straight out of the fridge and you're stuck whisking cold eggs that will probably never have the right lift to them.'

'I've never made one,' Ann said, struggling with a particularly stubborn pod. 'I've never really done very much cooking.' The pod split in half and the peas rolled across the kitchen floor with Ann in swift pursuit. 'No one ever lets me help,' Ann said, returning to her spot. 'I think they're afraid I'll have an accident.'

'Do you often have accidents?' Sister Ruth asked. A look at the clock confirmed that she needed to head over to the oven in five minutes for a quick peek.

'Usually only when I try to help after being told not to,' Ann replied guiltily. 'I really like to help!'

'Well, I certainly do need all the help I can get,' Sister Ruth smiled. 'So that shouldn't be a problem.' She stood up and wiped her hands down her apron. 'If you finish up with those peas, I'll get that soufflé out and let it stand.'

Ann continued to shell the peas, her lips twisted in concentration. 'I like your kitchen,' she said a short while later, with a filled bowl in front of her. 'It's very cosy.'

'Thank you!' Sister Ruth said, as she ran the tap to do the dishes. 'I quite enjoy being in here myself.' She lifted the blinds over the kitchen sink and wrinkled her nose at the grey skies outside. 'What would you like for dinner?' she asked brightly, turning around to smile at Ann. 'I'll let you pick whatever you want.'

'Sausages,' Ann replied promptly. 'Sausages and mash.'

'Oh,' Sister Ruth looked slightly crestfallen. 'Oh dear.'

'Are you out of sausages?' Ann asked. 'It doesn't matter. We can have them another night.'

'I can't make them,' Sister Ruth said sadly, looking around her kitchen. 'I don't have the right equipment.'

'To fry sausages?' Ann looked puzzled. 'Can't you just use a regular frying pan?'

'I can't make the actual sausages,' Sister Ruth said, walking over to the wire cooling racks to check on her soufflé. 'I would need some sort of stuffing device. I've often wondered whether I should ask Sister Sparkplug to build me one, but I suspect I would end up with a sausage maker that tried to fry eggs instead.'

'Can't you just buy them?' Ann asked. 'Get them from somewhere else, I mean.'

'The pigeons can't be trusted with them,' Sister Ruth said, shaking her head firmly. 'Once they get their beaks into something, that's the end of any nice treat you'd hoped to make for yourself.' She stared wistfully at a magazine clipping of a plate of bacon that was pinned to the kitchen noticeboard. 'They poked holes into a small parcel of meat once while carrying it from the Sisters of the Sacred Farm,' she said. 'The meat was ruined and the silly birds were ill for two days as well, so no one enjoyed it in the end.' She sighed and headed over to the sink to do the remaining dishes.

'I mean from a shop in Pistachio,' Ann explained. 'It's just down the mountain.'

'Oh, we don't go down there,' Sister Ruth said over her shoulder as she rinsed out a saucepan. 'Didn't the Reverend Mother tell you? It's not safe at all.'

'But where do you get your bread from?' Ann asked, looking at the pile of golden brown loaves on the kitchen table. 'Isn't that from the town?'

'Why, of course not!' exclaimed Sister Ruth. 'I make it myself, with these old paws here.' She held her soapy hands up to Ann, grinning widely. 'We have a small crop of wheat growing just outside the back garden and a very large sack of flour in the pantry. We do everything we can on our own here, and go without anything that we can't make ourselves.'

'I've never seen anyone make bread before,' Ann said, slightly awestruck. 'All the other abbeys just bought theirs from the nearby towns.' She reached out to touch the crinkled tops of the crusty bread. 'Is it very hard to make bread?'

'I'll call you over the next time I have a baking day,' Sister Ruth promised, rinsing a stainless steel pan and smiling at her own reflection in it. 'Now you run along and have some fun. Nothing dangerous, mind!'

'I found a ball in one of the cupboards the other day,' said Ann, heading out of the side door into the garden. 'Sister Pauline said I could try teaching Bonjour! how to play fetch. I think this could be interesting!' Sister Ruth made an unintelligible sound that signified exactly what she thought of the little guinea pig and returned to washing her dishes.

***

Teaching Bonjour! to play fetch in the back garden was more complicated than Ann had thought because he decided that he wanted to go visit the chicken coop instead. Ann had to quickly put him on his tiny leash, as she was fairly certain the chickens would think he was some sort of furry edible treat. She tied the end of the leash to the garden bench and rolled the ball away from him, trying to get him to follow it. Bonjour!, however, decided that playing with a ball was beneath him and curled up on the corner of the bench to sleep instead.

'Oh no,' Ann sighed as the ball rolled under the gates of the abbey and headed down the side of the mountain. She checked that Bonjour!'s leash was secure, then quietly stepped out through the gate and latched it behind her, looking up at the windows of the abbey to make sure no one was watching. Ann walked through the trees and to the edge of the mountain and peered down. She could see the red rubber ball caught in a gorse bush halfway down the grassy slope. Rolling her sleeves up and tying her hair back, Ann began to carefully climb down, her nimble feet quickly stepping from stone hold to stone hold until she reached the ball.

Ann could see a dirt road in the distance below that wound its way down to the village. Settling down on a piece of jutting-out rock beside the bush, Ann tossed her ball into the air and caught it again as she watched birds fly over the peaceful rooftops of Pistachio. The silence was suddenly shattered by the unmistakable sound of a horse-drawn cart and a man having trouble with his horses. 'Turn left!' Ann heard him shout. 'No, not that way! We're going to the next town, not back home!'

'Hello there!' Hidden behind the bush, Ann heard a second man call out from a distance. 'A little trouble with the horses, I see?'

'Aye, they're being stubborn today,' the first man said, laughing. 'They're having a touch of the Monday blues and don't want to go to work! How's everything down at the mill?'

'Just making my way home after the early morning shift,' said the second man, who now sounded like he'd caught up. 'I think I'm having a touch of the Monday blues myself!'

'What's happening here?' Ann could now hear the voice of a third man, much gruffer and sterner than the other two. 'Isn't there work to be done?'

'I'm on my way out to make a delivery,' the first man said, sounding instantly less cheerful. 'Just leaving now.' The clip-clop of the horses started up again.

'I'm going home,' the second man added quietly. 'Good day, everyone.'

Once they were safely down the road and everything was quiet again, Ann emerged from behind the bush with her rubber ball. She climbed carefully up the mountain towards the abbey again, very intrigued about this mysterious town that the nuns seemed to be so afraid of.

8

'So aren't you even the tiniest bit curious about what's down in the town?' Ann asked one afternoon a few days later, as she helped Sister Ruth make her special chicken stew for dinner. The kitchen table was a colourful mess of chopped vegetables and little jars of spices with their lids off. 'Have you never wanted to go there for a quick visit?'

'Down to Pistachio?' Sister Ruth paused her methodical slicing of potatoes to wrinkle her nose. 'No, not really. Like I said the other day, it's far too dangerous.'

'But they could have restaurants with wonderful food!' Ann said insistently. 'You could be missing out on learning some great new recipes.'

'That may be,' Sister Ruth said, putting her knife down and popping a cherry tomato into her mouth. 'But I'd rather be safe than sorry.'

'The nuns at my last abbey would go to the Chinese restaurant in the next town every Saturday for dinner,' Ann said. 'They used to have fortune cookies and the people there were lots of fun. Once, they even had a man wearing a cupcake suit singing for the customers.'

'That sounds simply awful,' Sister Ruth said. 'He could have been hiding all sorts of weapons in that suit.'

'It was perfectly safe,' Ann insisted. 'Nothing bad ever happened.'

'Could you please pass me the garlic salt?' Sister Ruth asked as she rubbed her hands down the front of her apron and took a seat at the big kitchen table. She pulled the bowl of chicken towards her and began to season it with easy, practised strokes. The bird had been picked carefully from the flock of chickens that the nuns kept in a large wired coop at the far end of the garden, away from the loft where the pigeons lived. They didn't think it was a good idea for the flying and flightless birds to mix—Sister Beatrice was convinced that it would put ideas into the chickens' heads.

Ann picked up each little spice jar, squinting at each handwritten label until she found the right one. 'There isn't much left,' she said, shaking it.

Sister Ruth reached for the jar and shook her head at it sadly. 'I've been so careful with it,' she said. 'It took those three pigeons so long to fly here with my last bag of spices. Now they absolutely refuse to go on spice runs any more—makes them sneeze something terrible. They take one look at the carrying bag and stick their heads under their wings.'

'Where do your spices come from?' asked Ann, absently fingering the label on a carton of stock cubes.

The box was almost empty, with two solitary cubes at the bottom, nested in their golden foil wrappers. 'You're almost out of chicken stock as well,' she added.

'The abbey over the river,' replied Sister Ruth. 'The Convent of Infrequent Laughter. They have a local trader who comes around there with wares every month. Sister Frances, who runs the kitchen, has an agreement with me. I send her some of our lovely produce every now and then, and she sends the birds back with some goodies of her own.' She pointed at a small package on a shelf across the room. 'That's a slice of my good pound cake, wrapped and ready to go the next time the birds fancy a trip.' Sister Ruth picked a flat metal tray up from beside the sink and dusted a fine layer of flour off it. 'Can you put this on the shelf for me, please?'

Ann grabbed the tray in both hands and looked at it curiously. 'There's something written on the other side,' she remarked, putting it down on the kitchen table. 'To the Brave Nuns with the Deepest Gratitude from the Grateful Town of Pistachio,' Ann read as she traced each letter with her finger.

'Oh, that was a gift,' Sister Ruth waved dismissively, arranging the sliced potatoes around the chicken. 'From when the old Assassin Nuns prevented those bank robbers from making away with all the town's valuables.'

'Oooh, what did they do?' Ann sat down and looked at Sister Ruth eagerly. 'How did they catch them?'

'They scaled up the side of the building with grappling hooks and those night-vision things,' Sister Ruth said, wiping her hands down the sides of her apron and carrying the dish of marinated chicken to the oven. 'Four floors they climbed in the dead of the night. They had arrows with them and shot the bags of money right off the backs of those nasty bandits as they tried to escape.'

'What did they do with the thieves?' Ann asked.

'Tied them up nice and tight,' Sister Ruth replied. 'They left them there for the bank tellers to find the next day with a helpful note explaining what had happened. The townspeople were so pleased they presented the nuns a lovely plaque, which now works excellently as a kneading board for me,' she smiled cheerily at Ann.

'That's amazing!' Ann said, running a hand over the engravings on the plaque. 'You're proper heroes!'

'Not us,' Sister Ruth shook her head. 'It was a long time ago.'

'I'm sure the townspeople still love you,' Ann remarked. 'You should really go down there sometime. They might give you more free things!'

'We don't do any of that any more,' Sister Ruth said firmly. 'None of this life-risking nonsense for me, thank you!'

Ann wiped down the counter, carefully rubbing out any greasy spots she might have made. Sister Ruth may have her faults, but a messy kitchen was not one of them. 'Can I go help Sister Sparkplug now?' she asked, swaying back and forth on the balls of her feet. 'She promised I could watch her work on a new invention.'

'Off you go,' Sister Ruth said, dropping the chicken into the pan. 'And you tell Sister Sparkplug to keep that contraption of hers away from my kitchen.'

'Vroom likes you!' Ann laughed as she took her apron off and folded it over the chair. 'He just always wants to see how you are, that's all.'

'I'm happier when he's not making a mess in my kitchen,' Sister Ruth retorted, shaking her head at Ann as she skipped through the kitchen doors.

***

Later that day, the nuns were sitting around the dinner table, halfway through their meal, when the topic of the robot broom came up again.

'Vroom's been having a few more issues,' Sister Sparkplug said, spearing a piece of chicken with a fork and staring gloomily at it. 'Some of his wiring has come loose and my old screwdriver isn't as sharp as it used to be. I've patched him up with some tape for now, but it won't hold for very long.'

'It's the same thing with my rake,' Sister Parsnip said. 'A few of the prongs have broken and now it takes twice as long to get anything done. Ann and I had to pick up a basketful of dried leaves with our hands yesterday. Our hands!' She shook her head. 'All that time wasted when we could have been singing to the carrots. They do need some music while they're growing.'

'Singing?' Sister Mildew said suddenly, but Sister Agnes quickly put another portion of potatoes on her plate to distract her.

'If you want a new rake for your precious vegetable patch, you should go get one yourself,' Sister Beatrice said. 'I don't see you ever volunteering to head down to the town for supplies!'

'I don't see you volunteering either,' Sister Ruth interrupted, poking at the plate of leftover roast potatoes. 'And you're always going on about tools for your garden.' She was already planning the next day's lunch. A nice Spanish tortilla with the leftover spuds would be perfect, and maybe some of Sister Parsnip's fresh blueberries for dessert.

'I'll do it!' Ann said suddenly. She looked up to find the table of nuns staring back at her. 'I mean it. I'll go down to Pistachio to buy some supplies for you.'

'To Pistachio?' Sister Sparkplug's eyes widened. 'You want to go into the town?'

'Would you really?' Sister Ruth beamed. 'I could make you a list. There are quite a lot of extras that we could do with.' She bustled out of the room with an empty casserole dish and a wide grin across her face, already making up elaborate shopping lists in her head.

Ann sat up excitedly. 'Do you think they have a library? I'm sure they do. I've finished rereading all my favourite books and I really need something new now.'

'But we've never been down to Pistachio,' Sister Parsnip leaned back and crossed her arms. 'This just doesn't seem right to me, sending the child there all on her own.'

The Reverend Mother exchanged an uneasy glance with Sister Agnes. 'I think maybe we should find an alternate solution,' she said slowly. 'There's no point jumping into something potentially dangerous. Maybe we could breed stronger pigeons that could carry bigger things.'

'I wonder whether I need a letter from someone to register at the library,' Ann continued, unperturbed. 'You're my guardians, aren't you?' She looked at the nuns around the table. 'Can I get a note from you saying that it's okay for me to join the library?'

'No, Ann,' Sister Pauline said, her face filled with concern. 'You must not go to the town. I have this—how do you say it—this bad feeling inside.'

'But there's so much we need,' Ann insisted. 'You told me the other day that Bonjour! doesn't like to eat oats any more. Maybe I could find him some sort of guinea pig food at the pet shop instead.'

'But he will learn to eat something else!' Sister Pauline looked distressed. 'Please do not go out into the danger because of him.'

'Hymns!' Sister Mildew said happily. 'We should have an evening of hymns tonight.' The nuns groaned in unison. 'The old ones,' she continued. 'I have my old Latin hymn books somewhere. We can have the traditional five-hour service.'

'Oh dear,' said Sister Agnes. 'Shall we save it for something special instead, Sister Mildew? Maybe next Christmas?'

'We can have another one at Christmas,' said Sister Mildew stubbornly. 'You promised me an evening of hymns but it never happened. We have to do it tonight.' She pointed at Ann. 'You can help me. Didn't I teach you some Latin?'

Ann started to speak but Sister Parsnip waved at her to be quiet. Reaching out with the salad tongs, Sister Parsnip tapped a mug covered with Christmas trees on the shelf by the door. The mug instantly broke out into a tinny rendition of 'Away In A Manger'. Sister Mildew stopped mid-sentence and smiled vacantly. 'Oh, I like that song,' she said. Swaying back and forth slightly, she leaned back and closed her eyes.

'Works every single time,' Sister Parsnip whispered to Ann, putting the salad tongs back on the table.

***

The next day after breakfast, the nuns lined up at the downstairs window to reluctantly wave Ann goodbye as she stepped through the gates that separated them from the terrifying world outside. Sister Ruth had insisted on packing two sandwiches for Ann—one cheese and tomato, and the other with a generous spread of onion chutney—just in case something terrible happened. She also popped a handful of cherries and a shiny apple into Ann's bag just before she left. Sister Ruth was of the opinion that an extra portion of food would solve any problem one might face. She was not altogether wrong.

The Reverend Mother and Sister Sparkplug stood at the front door watching Ann leave, with Vroom between them, buzzing sporadically. Sister Beatrice was sitting in a flowerbed, shaking her head in disapproval as she weeded her begonia patch. She had attempted to talk Ann out of going that morning but the girl had been too excited to listen. Sister Agnes and Sister Parsnip waved their little handkerchiefs at Ann through the window, shouting out their goodbyes from a safe distance.

Sister Mildew, on the other hand, had to be sternly told off for trying to climb out of the window to join Ann on her little trip. At some point during breakfast, she'd misheard a part of the conversation and thought that Ann was on her way to meet the Pope. Assuming—rather correctly—that as the oldest person in the abbey, she should be the person representing the abbey, Sister Mildew had spent the rest of the morning trying to sneak past the other nuns and hide behind Ann. She was finally deposited in an armchair next to Sister Parsnip, who was under strict instructions to pounce on her if she tried to move.

Ann paused at the other side of the gates and waved at the nuns. 'Don't worry!' she said brightly. 'I'll be back before it gets too dark.' She walked away through the trees, stopping every now and then to turn around and wave at the nuns.

'Maybe I should have made her one more sandwich,' Sister Ruth said anxiously. 'There were a few leftover bits of roast chicken that would have been lovely between a some rye.'

'The girl has enough food on her to feed a small family,' said Sister Beatrice, who was now back inside, carrying a bunch of lilies from her garden. 'I'm sure she'll be fine.' But despite her words, a tiny frown tugged at the corners of her mouth.

'I've been waiting to go see the Pope for years,' scowled Sister Mildew. 'Then you go and send the elf instead.'

'The Pope isn't here, Sister Mildew,' Sister Parsnip said patiently. 'And she's not an elf, she's a child.'

Sister Mildew's eyes widened. 'What happened to the Pope?'

'Where's that musical mug?' Sister Sparkplug said wearily. 'Somebody please go get it.' She set the controls on Vroom to do a bit of light sweeping and then watched in dismay as he attempted to dismantle himself instead. 'Oh, you poor dear. Don't you worry, Ann will be back soon with a nice new screwdriver and I'll fix you right up again. How long did she say she'd be, Reverend Mother?' The Reverend Mother still stood looking out of the window, one hand absently playing with the sash. 'Reverend Mother,' repeated Sister Sparkplug. 'Is something wrong?'

The Reverend Mother looked as though she still hadn't heard her, but then finally turned around. 'I've remembered what it was that was bothering me,' she said. 'We haven't had an invitation to Pistachio's Winter Festival yet.'

'Oh,' said Sister Sparkplug. 'Maybe they forgot?'

'They've never forgotten before,' she replied. 'Not once. Even the year we had the only hailstorm this town has seen in the last fifty years.'

'Maybe they've all moved,' suggested Sister Beatrice. 'Some people suddenly decide to relocate on a whim, and do it with all their neighbours. I've read about it—it's a strange phenomenon.' She spoke in the unwavering tone of someone who is clearly making up the story that they're telling.

'Oh no!' exclaimed Sister Ruth. 'Has Ann gone down to a deserted town then?'

'They're all still there,' Sister Beatrice said. 'I see the smoke from their chimneys when I'm out hanging the laundry to dry.'

'Something's just not right,' the Reverend Mother said, reluctantly turning away from the window. 'I don't know what it is, but I can feel it in my bones.' Vroom spluttered as if to agree, and then promptly fell over in a pile on the carpet.

9

While the Assassin Nuns were trying to convince themselves that there was nothing wrong with the town of Pistachio, Ann was heading straight to the heart of the problem. With a bag slung over one shoulder and an apple in her hand, she cheerfully marched down the mountain, tunelessly humming one of the songs she'd heard at the abbey earlier that week.

Not being an official member of the abbey meant that Ann didn't really have to go to the chapel with them, but she'd chosen to wake up and sleepily join the other nuns for early morning prayers anyway. There was something about being able to sing as loudly as you wanted that made her quite happy. Sister Mildew, who was a big fan of long choruses and pretended to be deaf when anyone protested, was in charge of choosing the daily hymns, much to the other nuns' dismay. The Reverend Mother had put her in charge of the chapel because she wasn't very good at helping Sister Ruth in the kitchen and neither the chickens nor the pigeons seemed to like her very much. After she had killed Sister Parsnip's beloved tomato plants by accidentally watering them with motor oil, the Reverend Mother decided that it would be safest if Sister Mildew stayed away from the garden, and if that meant everyone spent an hour each morning trying to pronounce Latin lyrics correctly, then so be it.

As Ann sang a slightly wonky version of one of these hymns to herself, she reached the spot halfway down the mountain where she'd first spotted the town the day she had arrived. 'Oh my,' she said to herself as she bit into her apple with gusto. Pistachio looked beautiful, with its houses clustered together in the valley and their green tiled roofs almost merging with the trees that surrounded them. Still, a part of Ann was slightly disappointed, since she'd expected a lot more. Pistachio looked like a wonderful little town and the perfect place to live, but it just looked so very regular. After listening to the nuns' fears of the outside world, Ann had secretly hoped for something more exciting.

Ann took the last bite of her apple and scuffed at the ground with her shoe until she'd made a sizeable hole. She carefully dropped the core into the hole and covered it up with dirt. 'That's another apple tree for the world,' she announced happily to no one in particular. Having given Nature a kind boost, Ann continued on her way down the mountain. The road ahead of her forked sharply, one leading to the bus stop where Sister Agnes picked her up and the other presumably to the town. Ann stood there for a second, feeling more like an explorer

than ever. 'Onward, ho!' she said aloud, marching down the last leg of the mountain towards Pistachio. 'For truth and honour and the spirit of exploration!'

A narrow dirt path snaked through a cornfield with stalks so tall, Ann had to squint at the sky to see the tops of them. 'Perfect,' she said to herself. 'It's stealth mode now!' She made her way through the corn, careful not to snag her hair on any of the broken stalks, until she reached a large wooden sign at the bottom of the field. Ann looked up at the sign and frowned. The sign had originally read 'Welcome to Pistachio!' in big bold letters with a cheerful note underneath saying 'We're the happiest people you'll ever meet!' Now Ann was definitely a fan of cheerful people and always enjoyed a good laugh, so this wasn't what disturbed her. The thing that had made her stop was that the word 'NOT' had been scratched into the wood after the first word of the second line. Ann felt a tingle in her knees as she reached for her notebook. *Further inspection proves interesting. Definitely something going on here.* Ann tossed her hair back and headed straight into Pistachio.

The paved path wound past several houses with neat gardens and tightly shuttered windows and as Ann made her way to the heart of the town, her first impression of Pistachio was that it was very quiet. Now, Ann had been through many towns during her travels from one abbey to another, and there was usually a certain amount of chatter on the streets from people passing through, dogs barking at invisible enemies and friendly bicycle bells as cyclists rode past you. Pistachio, however, was dead silent.

Up ahead, Ann spied a small corner shop with a sign that read 'Pistachio Newsagents'. She walked in and was immediately struck by the strong smell of musty leather. The shop was badly lit and fitted with wooden shelves containing an assortment of newspapers, sweets, sandwiches, cans of cola and the other regular fare found in such small establishments. There was a pile of broken furniture against one wall and the whole place had an air of abandonment to it. The shop owner appeared to be missing and a disinterested green bird sat in a cage that hung behind the till. Squinting at the walls, she soon realized that the unpleasant smell came from what looked like a collection of ageing horse saddles hung up in three neat rows. Despite the powerful smell, Ann couldn't help but step closer for a better look.

'Something I can help you with, little girl?'

Ann jumped, startled at the booming voice that seemed to come out of nowhere. 'Hello?' she said warily, looking around for someone else in the shop.

'Over here,' continued the voice. 'By the window.' Ann turned around and an old man in a wheelchair emerged from the shadows. The bird chose this exact moment to let out a high-pitched squawk, causing Ann to jump again. 'Quiet, Zeus!' The old man frowned at the cage. He turned towards Ann again and began to make his way across the room to her, his gnarled hands turning the wheels. 'Apologies for the bird, m'dear,' he said. 'She's not very used to strangers.'

'That's okay,' Ann said, shrugging her shoulders. 'Birds don't like me very much anyway.'

'Is that true now?' The old man was now almost in front of her. His face was covered in a series of criss-crossed lines that made it look rather like an old map.

'Oh yes,' said Ann merrily. 'Sister Fleur once had a budgie who would scream every time it saw me. I think it was my hair.' She looked up, slightly cross-eyed, at the offending tendrils that were starting to escape from her braid. 'Not plain old bird screams,' she added with relish. 'Proper screams like people being killed. Blood-curdling.'

'Ah, you must be from the abbey then,' the old man nodded his head slightly. 'I haven't seen any of you lot down here in years. What happened? Did the building fall apart?'

'The abbey's just fine,' Ann replied. 'I'm just here to do some shopping and drop some vegetables off at the market.' She held her basket of Sister Parsnip's finest produce up for inspection. 'I'm Ann, by the way,' she added, offering him her hand. 'I'm new.'

'Aye, you must be new,' the old man said, shaking her hand with a surprisingly firm grip. 'None of these nuns would ever come down here and mingle with the likes of us.' He shook his head at her. 'They think they're too good for this town, don't they, Zeus?' Zeus tucked his head under a wing and ignored his owner.

'I'm sure they don't feel that way,' Ann said quickly, trying to defend her new home. 'Maybe they just think you don't like them so they're staying away.'

'What's to like about them?' asked the old man grumpily. 'Don't see them enough to like them.'

'Why is it so quiet here?' Ann asked, still squinting at the saddles on the wall. 'Is there something happening today? Are people getting ready for a parade or something?'

'A parade? Not this town,' he said, looking away. 'No one does things like that here any more.'

'You haven't told me your name yet,' Ann said.

'They call me Old Joel,' he replied. 'I used to work at the stables, but then my back went out and now I sell newspapers instead.' He gestured at the saddles at Ann was looking at. 'Those are all from my prize horses,' he said proudly. 'I have a shelf full of trophies at home, too.'

'I've ridden a horse once,' Ann said thoughtfully. 'It was a very bumpy experience. It was on a beach trip with the Sisters of Occasional Benevolence and a seagull stole my ice cream.'

'Birds are nasty critters,' Old Joel agreed, shaking his head at the parrot. 'Isn't that right, Zeus?'

'Nasty! Nasty!' the parrot squawked loudly as it shuffled across its perch. 'Nasty!'

'So what's all this shopping you need to do?' Old Joel asked, wheeling himself over to the till. 'Anything I can help you with?'

'I need some sausages,' Ann said. 'And a rake and a screwdriver.' She pulled the list out of her pocket and skimmed over it. 'Lots of other things as well,' she said finally.

'Oh, you won't get any of that from here,' he said. 'You want to head over to the grocer's, to Mr Morris. That's just down—' Old Joel paused suddenly and held a finger out, motioning Ann to be quiet. He listened intently for a few seconds and then relaxed. 'Never mind,' he said. 'I thought I heard that awful car outside. I was saying, the shop you want is down the road, straight on for a few more minutes.'

'What car?' Ann asked curiously, as she headed for the door.

'Never mind all that,' Old Joel said. 'Off you go to finish your shopping. You don't want to be here when it gets dark.'

Ann stepped back outside, the fresh air reminding her how musty the shop had been. In the distance, she saw a woman headed towards her, her hair tied back in a red scarf and the heels of her shoes clicking against the paved road as she walked. 'Hello,' Ann called out as the woman got closer. 'How are you?'

The woman looked uncomfortable and smiled nervously. 'Hello,' she said, brushing a strand of hair off her face. 'Shouldn't you be at school?'

'It's the weekend, plus I have my lessons at the abbey,' Ann replied, gesturing vaguely in the direction of the mountain. 'My name's Ann.'

'I'm Mrs Potter,' the woman replied, her eyes darting behind Ann. 'I really should be on my way. I'm late for my shift.'

'It was very nice meeting you,' Ann said, but the woman was already walking away briskly. 'That's odd,' Ann said to herself, as she continued to head into the town. 'That's very odd indeed.'

Up ahead, Ann could see the shop that Old Joel had mentioned. It was a big white building with large glass windows filled with displays of fruit, vegetables and canned goods. As she stepped through the doors, a bell above her head tinkled.

'Why, hello there!' A short, red-faced man made his way towards Ann, a toothy grin spreading across his face. 'Now who do we have here?'

'Hello,' said Ann politely. 'I'm from the abbey.'

Mr Morris laughed. 'Aren't you a little young to be a nun?'

'I'm not a nun,' said Ann. 'I just live there and help them with things.' She hoisted her basket up onto the counter. 'Would you be interested in buying some of these?' She held up a tomato. 'They're all very good.'

'That's all quite lovely,' Mr Morris beamed, looking at Sister Parsnip's beautiful vegetables. 'Really, really lovely. They're going to get snapped up like this!' He snapped his fingers to demonstrate. 'Now, what can I help you with?'

'I need a few things,' Ann said, carefully unfolding the list Sister Ruth had given her earlier that day. 'Some provisions and tools and definitely some bacon.'

'I'll let you have a wander around then,' said Mr Morris said pleasantly. He reached behind the counter and handed her a large plastic basket. 'For your shopping,' he added. 'Just pop in what you want and I'll add up how much I owe you for the vegetables. We'll work out a nice exchange.' He winked at Ann happily.

Ann wandered through the shop, picking up everything that the nuns had asked for—from gardening tools to frozen shrimp—and also slipped in a few things she thought they might enjoy. 'Which do you think I should get?' she shouted out to Mr Morris. 'Jellybeans or chocolate buttons?'

'I'm a chocolate button man myself,' Mr Morris said, coming over. 'But those are some lovely jellybeans. Wonderful flavours.'

'I think I'll get both,' Ann said, dropping them into her basket and heading towards the till. 'That way I won't have to decide!'

As Mr Morris totalled and bagged her shopping, Ann stood at the window looking out at the empty streets of Pistachio. 'Where's everyone?' she asked. 'I've seen hardly anyone outside today.'

'At work,' Mr Morris said, putting the last tin of baked beans in and bringing the shopping bags over to Ann. 'There you go, all nicely bagged.'

'But it's the weekend!' Ann said. 'Why do they work on weekends?' She picked up a paper bag in each hand. 'Thank you,' she added.

'I didn't realize it was a weekend,' Mr Morris said, rubbing his head as he headed back to the till. 'Don't really notice them any more. Time just flies.'

'Oh, one more thing,' Ann stopped at the doorway and turned around. 'Is there a children's library here? Any library would do, really. I'd like to become a member now that I'm living in the abbey.'

Mr Morris looked at her with an unreadable expression in his eyes. 'No,' he said finally. 'There's no library in Pistachio.'

'A bookshop will do as well,' Ann said, putting her bags down and pushing her unruly hair back. 'I'm running out of things to read!'

'We don't have one of those either.' Mr Morris looked away, suddenly busying himself with the till.

'Oh,' said Ann, slightly taken aback. 'Isn't that a little strange?' Mr Morris, however, had now disappeared completely behind the till and Ann realized that it was as much as she was going to get out of him today. Carrying the bags of shopping in both hands and her bag slung across her chest, Ann stepped out onto the road to head back the way she'd come.

Ann kept her eyes peeled on the way out, but it appeared as though Mr Morris was telling the truth. There was not a single bookshop in sight.

10

'And you're absolutely certain that you're alright?' Sister Ruth asked for the third time, as she brought Ann a bowl of steaming cauliflower soup. Ann was seated at one end of the kitchen table munching on a slice of bread, opposite an old-fashioned oil lamp that cast spindly shadows across the walls. The Reverend Mother and Sister Agnes sat on either side on her, dressed in long white nightgowns and their hair in long braids. Ann hadn't seen them without their wimples before and had to stop herself from staring.

Somewhat distracted by her dinner, Ann nodded with her mouth full. 'Ngffbffr,' she said, reaching for a spoon and wondering whether to dive into the soup and risk the possibility of a burned mouth.

'What was that?' the Reverend Mother asked politely.

'Never better,' repeated Ann, brushing the crumbs off her mouth with the back of her hand. 'Sorry,' she added. 'I'm very hungry.'

'Good,' said Sister Ruth, passing her another slice of bread. 'Now you tell us everything about that town right away.' She settled down at the table with a cup of cocoa. 'After that, I'm going to put the provisions away.' Packages containing various things for the kitchen were piled up on the counter. The other things from the list had been given to each of the delighted nuns who'd asked for them and the general atmosphere around the abbey was a lot like Christmas.

Before Ann could begin, Sister Sparkplug wandered into the kitchen with a frayed wire in one hand and a pair of pliers in the other. Vroom came in from behind her and sped into the room, buzzing excitedly and trailing a thin stream of what looked like treacle across the floor. 'HeffoVfffom,' Ann managed as she waved at him. The robot broom stopped next to Ann and leaned forward, tapping her on the arm with his handle. 'You look lovely,' she said, patting him admiringly. 'So nice and shiny.'

'Oil!' squealed Sister Ruth in agitation. 'There's oil on my beautiful, spotless floor! I just finished cleaning the whole place!'

'Oh dear,' said Sister Sparkplug. 'I'm terribly sorry. He's just excited because he's had some repairing done.' She felt around in her pockets and pulled out an oil-stained rag. 'I'll sort the floor out right away, don't worry.'

Sister Ruth rolled her eyes and took a sip of her cocoa. 'Stupid machine,' she muttered under her breath.

'That was a fine screwdriver you picked up for me, Ann,' Sister Sparkplug smiled widely, pulling it out of her pocket. 'Such a lovely, top-class piece of equipment.' She waved it in the air as she knelt down on the floor to clean up Vroom's little accident. Ann took another bite of her bread and stretched down again to pat the errant machine, which had now neatly folded itself up in a pile under her chair and was whirring contently.

'Is Vroom all fixed up now?' asked Sister Agnes, eyeing Ann's soup and telling herself that she didn't need another snack right after dinner, even though the tantalizing smell of cauliflower and cheese seemed like too much to resist.

'Just a bit of a leakage problem,' said Sister Sparkplug, as she shot an apologetic look at Sister Ruth. 'But other than that, he's better!' She finished rubbing at the stain on the floor and positioned herself over it, hoping Sister Ruth wouldn't notice that it hadn't completely disappeared from the floorboards.

Sister Ruth snorted as she finished up the last of her cocoa and put her mug in the sink. 'The next time he makes a mess on my floor, I'm going to ban him from ever entering the kitchen again,' she said, 'and I mean it.'

Sister Parsnip stepped into the kitchen, examining the new set of gardening tools Ann had brought back, with Sister Beatrice behind her. 'I didn't think you'd make it back,' Sister Beatrice said gloomily. 'I hope you haven't brought back some terrible disease that you're going to give to the rest of us now.'

'We really should have sent someone down there years ago with a shopping list,' Sister Sparkplug said, still admiring her screwdriver. 'If I'd had the right tools back then, I might have even been able to save the boot dryer and the egg counter.'

'What was the boot dryer?' Ann asked curiously.

'Never mind the boot dryer,' Sister Agnes cut in before Sister Sparkplug could begin her explanation. 'Tell us about your trip.' She slipped over to the stove and helped herself to a small portion of soup.

Ann scraped up the remnants of cauliflower and licked her spoon dry. 'There's no library,' she started. 'There's no bookshop either. How can a town have no bookshop?' She looked aghast.

'Was there much violence?' Sister Parsnip asked anxiously. 'Did you have to defend yourself?'

'There weren't many people around,' Ann said. 'Everyone seemed to be busy at work even though it's a weekend.'

'What about the restaurants?' asked Sister Ruth wistfully. 'What are the restaurants like? Did you happen to look at any of the menus?'

Ann scrunched her face as she tried to remember. 'I don't think I saw any restaurants on my way,' she said finally. 'Nothing looked open.'

'Don't be silly,' Sister Ruth said. 'Every town has at least one restaurant and Friday nights are always the busiest.'

'Every town has a library too!' Ann exclaimed. 'But Mr Morris said they didn't have one.' She spun her spoon around the empty bowl in front of her. 'He's the local grocer,' she added. 'He's nice.'

Sister Pauline wandered in with Bonjour! on her shoulder and joined the other nuns at the kitchen table. 'Hello, Ann,' she said, quickly putting the guinea pig in her pocket after catching sight of Sister Ruth's face. 'How did you enjoy your big adventure in Pistachio?'

'It was very good, thank you,' Ann replied, reaching into her pocket for a small packet. 'I didn't forget,' she said. 'They didn't have a lot for me to choose from, so I got rabbit pellets instead. I hope he likes them.'

'Rabbit is good,' Sister Pauline said happily. 'Rabbit is very good. Thank you so much!' She poured a few pellets into her hand and held them up to Bonjour!. The guinea pig sniffed at them and ate them quickly, clearly pleased with his new snack. 'Look!' Sister Pauline said. 'His appetite, it has come back!'

'I met a parrot named Zeus today as well,' Ann said. 'I don't think I like parrots very much.'

'I had a parrot as a child,' Sister Parsnip said, smiling. 'We really couldn't get him to shut up. When it got too much, we had to put a cloth over his cage so he thought it was night and would fall asleep. That was the only way we could get him to stop talking.'

'Parrots are vicious creatures,' Sister Beatrice said. 'Full of disease. I hope you've washed your hands thoroughly.' She moved her chair away from Ann.

'I didn't touch it,' Ann said. 'It belonged to an old man called Joel. He was in a wheelchair and said he remembered the old Assassin Nuns before you.'

'I remember that name,' Sister Agnes said slowly. 'I think he used to hire out cars or buses or something to the old nuns when they had to go somewhere. I've seen his name on some old paperwork.' She shrugged. 'It was a very long time ago.'

'I think he just runs a small shop now,' Ann said. 'It smelled like horses.'

'Horses!' Sister Agnes exclaimed, slapping her leg. 'That's what it was! They used to hire horses from him. Can't imagine why.'

'Terrible creatures, horses,' Sister Beatrice said. 'Riddled with disease.'

'I didn't touch anything,' Ann said quickly. 'And Sister Agnes already made me take two showers in case I picked up some terrible germs.'

'They did use the horses to get around,' the Reverend Mother nodded. 'I remember them riding up to the abbey after they'd been out fighting.' She shuddered slightly. 'Such dangerous creatures, those horses.'

'Bacon for breakfast tomorrow!' Sister Ruth said excitedly, as she started to unpack the shopping. 'I never thought we'd have bacon again.'

'Did the town seem alright?' the Reverend Mother asked. 'No trouble or disturbance anywhere?'

'It was very quiet,' Ann said. 'And everyone I met was very nice. One lady was in a bit of a hurry, but the others were very helpful.'

'Have they started setting up for the Winter Festival?' Sister Agnes asked. 'It's usually around this time of the year.

I always imagined they'd have lots of bunting everywhere, with balloons and fairy lights.'

'And the food stalls,' Sister Ruth said as she put some of her new tins away. 'The invitation always talks about the food stalls. Did they have those up yet?'

'There was nothing up,' Ann said, shaking her head. 'The streets were empty and no one mentioned anything about a Winter Festival.'

'That's strange,' Sister Parsnip said. 'Maybe it's next month instead.'

'What's strange is that there was no library,' Ann said, slightly disgruntled. 'I was really looking forward to getting some new books!'

'I'll have a look around,' Sister Agnes promised, stifling a yawn. 'I'll see if I can find you something in the attic. I'm sure we have books you can read somewhere.'

'Since we're all awake now,' the Reverend Mother said, standing up and heading for the door, 'I suggest we go to the chapel for evening prayers before we go to bed.' She stopped to do a quick headcount. 'Let's not bother waking Sister Mildew,' she said quickly. 'We'll just have a quick one tonight with no singing.'

***

'So do you think this is a good idea?' Sister Agnes asked the Reverend Mother as they settled down for a late night hot chocolate in the front room. The other nuns had retired for the night and all the lights were turned off except for a small lamp in the corner. 'This whole business makes me feel uneasy. We've been perfectly fine staying in the abbey and living off what we have for the last few years. Now, just as it looks like there may be something wrong in the town, we've decided to start sending Ann down there to do our shopping.' She shook her head fiercely. 'It just doesn't feel right.'

'I'm sure there's nothing wrong,' the Reverend Mother said. 'From what Ann said, it seems to be business as usual in Pistachio. It's probably just some sort of misunderstanding.' She paused to take a sip of her drink. 'By the time the old nuns left, there wasn't any crime left to deal with. The town's been perfectly safe since then.'

Both the nuns were silent for the next few minutes as they listened to the chirping sounds of the crickets outside. 'I thought of something when I was in evening prayers just now,' Sister Agnes said suddenly, blowing on her steaming mug. 'Not that I wasn't paying attention,' she said hurriedly, before the Reverend Mother could protest. 'I was paying attention, but then I started to wonder about something Ann said. Pistachio does have a library and at least one restaurant—they're always mentioning them in the invitations every year. The parade starts at the library and the restaurant owners always have some sort of food stand at the town centre.'

'I didn't realize you read those so carefully,' the Reverend Mother said, slightly surprised. 'Or that you had such a good memory. You're right, though. That's quite peculiar.'

'They also definitely have a bookshop,' Sister Agnes continued, closing her eyes as she tried to remember. 'They mentioned it in this summer's invitation. They had a special sale on to celebrate the Summer Festival.' She opened her eyes and looked at the Reverend Mother. 'Why would they all disappear now?'

'That is very strange,' the Reverend Mother agreed. 'Is it possible that Ann just missed seeing them?'

Sister Agnes snorted. 'That child would badger everyone she met until she found what she was looking for,' she said. 'If she says there's no bookshop, I believe her.'

'Most definitely odd,' the Reverend Mother repeated as she lifted her mug up to reach the last bittersweet dregs of her hot chocolate.

Later that night, tucked up in her warm bed, the Reverend Mother stared at the picture of her predecessor on the wall, illuminated by a shaft of moonlight. The Mother Superior had always been so sure of herself and been such an excellent leader. Suddenly, she felt ill-equipped to run the abbey after a series of wonderful and brave nuns before her. Maybe Sister Agnes was right, maybe there was something very wrong going on in Pistachio and maybe they ought to investigate. As she turned over to find a comfortable spot on her pillow, her mind was filled with all the terrible things that were likely happen if they left the abbey. 'They'll be fine,' she said to herself. 'The town will take care of itself.' And as she fell asleep, she almost believed it.

11

Ann stood outside the pigeon loft, which was a small wooden construction with several mesh-covered windows situated on one side of the back garden. She was wearing a pair of oversized orange polka-dot wellies she'd borrowed from Sister Sparkplug, and brandishing a very large rake. The pigeon loft was located next to Sister Beatrice's flowerbeds, and the bottom of the little building was set on blocks to keep it from sinking into the mud. Ann's feet made a loud squelching sound every time she moved, which she found endlessly fascinating.

'Right,' said Sister Agnes, appearing by her side with a bucket filled with straw and two pairs of long yellow rubber gloves. 'Let's get started, shall we?' She handed Ann a pair of gloves and pulled her own on. 'We don't want any of that muck down our fingernails,' she said, frowning with concentration as she tugged each finger into place. 'It takes absolutely forever to get the smell off your hands, trust me.'

Ann found the gloves a few sizes too big, but folded the ends over twice to keep them in place. 'What are we doing today?' she asked, lifting her foot up and putting it back down in the mud again with relish.

'We're on grunt duty,' Sister Agnes replied, tying her wimple into a knot. 'The loft needs cleaning, and it needs a real good cleaning too.' She shook her head and took a deep breath. 'Ready?' she asked Ann, and threw the door open before she could answer.

The smell was the first thing that struck Ann; the second was a tiny bird-shaped missile. 'Ow!' she said, rubbing the side of her head with a glove-covered hand. The offending pigeon strutted on the ground next to her, clearly pleased at his accurate aim.

'You'll need to watch out for the strays,' Sister Agnes shook her head sympathetically. 'There's always one in there, primed for an attack.'

Ann wrinkled her nose and gingerly stepped into the loft, keeping a lookout for any more violent pigeons. The walls were lined with little wooden compartments, just big enough for a grown bird to sit in, and the floor was covered with straw. A beam ran across one side, where a few roosting birds sat on their nests and stared at them suspiciously. A closer inspection of the straw on the ground revealed that it—and nearly every other surface—was covered in a layer of bird droppings.

'Does it always smell this bad?' Ann asked, looking at the mess on the floor and not certain that she wanted to step any further.

'It's not that smelly,' said Sister Agnes, pushing past her and pointing at a small stone birdbath in the corner. 'Pigeons are very clean. They'll wash themselves every day if you give them clean water, not like those smelly chickens!'

'The floor's still disgusting, though,' Ann observed.

'That's what we're here for!" Sister Agnes said brightly, motioning Ann forward. 'Now use that rake you have there to move all the dirty straw out of the way, and we'll replace it with the clean stuff I have in the bucket.' Ann stuck her rake out and started to gather the straw on the floor into a pile with broad strokes, quickly starting to enjoy the easy rhythm of the movements. The teeth made a pleasant sound against the straw and the wooden floor, and the roosting pigeons cooed as they watched her work. Sister Agnes observed her with a broad smile across her face. 'Nice, isn't it?' she said. 'Something very calming about cleaning this floor.'

Two pigeons hopped in from outside to investigate and Sister Agnes tugged a glove off and reached into her habit to pull out half a slice of bread. 'Off you go,' she said, tossing the bread outside the loft. The pigeons hopped back outside and began to fight over the bread, flapping their wings at each other violently. One of them eventually won, strutting across the path with his hard-earned prize, while the other stood there, looking at Sister Agnes accusingly.

'Run along, Hubert,' she said, waving him away. 'It's not my fault you weren't quick enough.' The pigeon flew into one of the boxes on the wall and continued to stare at them with beady eyes.

'Have you named all the birds?' Ann asked in surprise. 'They all look the same to me. How do you tell them apart?'

'Oh, I don't really,' said Sister Agnes with a laugh. 'They're all Hubert to me.' She passed another piece of bread to Ann. 'Here, have a go.'

'Hello, Hubert,' Ann said, pulling her gloves off and holding the bread out to him. The pigeon flew at her, wings flapping wildly, and grabbed at the bread with its claws. 'Owwww,' Ann said, waving her hand in the air. 'Pigeons don't like me.'

'Always best to drop it on the ground,' said Sister Agnes. 'They can get a little grabby.' She stood on tiptoe and took a peek at the pigeons sitting on their nests. 'That's nice,' she smiled. 'We'll have some little ones soon.'

Ann stepped out of the loft and breathed in a lungful of fresh air. 'That's so much better,' she said. 'I never thought I'd actually appreciate fresh air.'

'I could do with a nice pie and some chips,' said Sister Agnes said, following her outside and idly rubbing her belly. 'All this work really brings out my appetite.'

'I could do with a fish finger sandwich,' said Ann, sucking on her finger. 'With a bit of mayo on the side.'

'Fish finger sandwiches?' Sister Agnes looked incredulous. 'Fish fingers in sandwiches? Do people really eat them?'

'Oooh, they're lovely,' Ann said, her face scrunching up in delight. 'The Sisters of the Blessed Pier always had plenty of fish in the freezer, and whenever Sister Gertrude wanted to clear some room out for the next catch, she made a large batch of fish fingers that had to be eaten within the week.'

'Ah yes,' Sister Agnes nodded knowingly. 'Sister Ruth does that with her potato fritters. We have them with our meals every day until there's only a reasonable number of potatoes left in the pantry.'

'I used to have my fish fingers with some bread and ketchup,' Ann continued. 'Lovely, lovely, lovely!'

'We don't have any ketchup,' Sister Agnes said ruefully. 'It's too heavy for the birds to carry.' Hubert flew down to the ground next to them and cooed in agreement.

'Why haven't you just bought some from Pistachio?' Ann asked. 'I saw plenty of ketchup and mustard in the shop when I went there last week.'

'Oh no,' Sister Agnes shook her head. 'You're a lot braver than I am.' She checked her pockets and found a scrap of bread, which she tossed at Hubert. 'Terrible things happen in the outside world, you know. I'd rather just stay here.' She watched the pigeon scarf down his treat and hop about happily. 'It would be lovely to have a spot of Worcestershire sauce with me eggs, though,' she added dreamily. 'Just a tiny bit right on top of them.'

'It's a very nice town,' Ann persisted. 'Have you never been there?'

'Oh, not really,' said Sister Agnes. 'I passed through it when I first joined the abbey, though. I think it was one of their annual festivals and the people were very loud.' She cocked her head to the side as she tried to remember. 'Lots of music and noise,' she continued. 'And all these animals and children running around everywhere. Do you know how many accidents an unsupervised child can cause?'

'Children!' Ann said suddenly. 'That's what it was! There were no children playing that evening when I went there. Not a single one.' She looked up at Sister Agnes. 'Don't you think that's very odd? Possibly even odder than having no library.'

'Their parents probably realized it's safest to keep them indoors,' said Sister Agnes, pulling her gloves off slowly. 'So many terrible things happen outside.' She stuffed her gloves into the pocket of her habit and turned to Ann. 'They used to have a library, you know,' she said offhandedly. 'I was telling the Reverend Mother the other day that I'm sure they've mentioned it on their list of festival events before.'

'I knew there had to be one!' Ann exclaimed. 'Why do you think Mr Morris told me it was gone?'

Sister Agnes shrugged. 'People are strange,' she said. 'Maybe they just didn't want one any more.'

'It's all just very, very odd,' Ann said, her eyebrows knitting together in a frown. 'I really wonder what's going on down there.'

'Well, as long as it's not a tiger roaming about again, I'm sure everything's just fine,' Sister Agnes stretched her arms out and yawned.

'You know the story about the tiger?' Ann asked with wide eyes. 'The story of how the old Assassin Nuns dealt with a tiger?

'Sister Mildew told me all about it,' Sister Agnes replied. 'Back when she wasn't as . . . forgetful. She used to be one of them, you know.'

'One of the real Assassin Nuns?'

'We're real, too,' Sister Agnes protested, tossing another scrap of bread at one of the Huberts.

'Tell me about the tiger!' demanded Ann.

'Well,' Sister Agnes started. 'I do believe this was fifteen—no, twenty—years ago. There were rumours that an angry tiger had escaped from a zoo and was prowling the moors, but no one really believed them until someone saw it ripping up posters for the town festival. The nasty beast had made it halfway through Pistachio, terrorizing the local dogs and making a mess of people's gardens, when the nuns arrived. Two of them managed to wrestle it to the ground when—'

'The nuns wrestled with a tiger?' Ann's voice was tinged with amazement. 'Not really?'

'They did indeed,' Sister Agnes shook her head in disapproval. 'With their shields and not much else. Such a risky thing to do, don't you agree? Then the Mother Superior showed up with a lasso and some sausages and managed to get the animal to behave itself until the zookeepers came to take it away.'

'That's fantastic!' Ann exclaimed. 'Weren't they terrified?'

'There's a painting of it in the hallway,' Sister Agnes continued. 'Sister Hattie, Sister Regina and the tiger, mid-fight. No one thought to take a photograph, so one of the other nuns drew a picture the next day instead.'

'Is that the picture with the purple monster?' Ann asked, wrinkling her nose.

'That's the one,' Sister Agnes replied. 'I believe they'd run out of orange paint and had to make do with what they had left.'

'They wrestled a tiger,' Ann said dreamily. 'That's amazing.'

'You think so?' Sister Agnes looked doubtful. 'I think it's all rather disturbing.'

'I wish I knew how to wrestle a tiger,' Ann said. 'I think it's quite a useful skill to have.'

Sister Agnes, however, had lost all interest in tigers and the old Assassin Nuns. She pulled an old sack out from behind the pigeon loft, and used the rake to stuff the dirty straw into it. 'That's our afternoon task done,' she said happily. 'I think I need a bit of a lie-down now. Are you coming in as well, Ann?'

'I'll stay out here and watch the pigeons,' Ann replied. 'I have a French lesson coming up with Sister Pauline soon.' The various Huberts were now sitting in a row on the roof, cooing occasionally as they looked out down at the garden.

Ann stood in front of the loft after Sister Agnes left, absent-mindedly squelching her wellies in the mud, one boot after the other, as she imagined herself facing a whole pack of tigers. She was now almost certain that the lack of children and disappearing library in Pistachio were part of the strange goings-on that she couldn't quite put her finger on. Everyone she'd met in the town had seemed like they were always looking over their shoulder, almost like saying the wrong thing might get them into trouble. Even the lovely Mr Morris at the shop had seemed wary when she asked him about the town. Her concentration was broken by the sound of footsteps coming up the path. 'Hello,' said Sister Pauline cheerfully, coming up from behind her. 'They said you are in the *pigeonnier* so I come to find you.' Bonjour! scampered up her arm and sat on her shoulder, staring at Ann. 'How are you enjoying meeting the birds?'

'Pigeons are scary,' Ann said. 'They also have very sharp beaks.' She examined the scratch on her hand, secretly hoping that it would leave her with a lovely purple bruise. Ann didn't consider injuries worthwhile unless they left a mark of some sort.

'They are very tasty with beans,' Sister Pauline said thoughtfully. 'Not these other beans like you have with the toast, but the good green beans.' She nodded earnestly at Ann as she spoke. 'My mother, she used to make this for us when I was young. Sister Ruth, she only makes the chicken here. She says pigeon is only for the post.' Sister Pauline shook her head, clearly disagreeing with the culinary choices at the abbey.

'Were you really born in France?' Ann asked curiously. She stretched a hand out and patted Bonjour! gently on the head.

'Oui,' Sister Pauline smiled. 'I come from a very small village called Le Monestier.' Bonjour! sniffed at Ann's fingers, then crept into her outstretched hand. Sister Pauline looked on approvingly as Ann proceeded to fuss over him. 'It is near the town of Annonay,' she continued. 'That is where the brothers Montgolfier made the first *montgolfière*—no, how do you say it—the gas balloon that goes up, up, up.' Her eyes lit up as she stretched her arms out. 'When I was a little girl, I wanted to live in a balloon in the sky.'

'Ooooh,' Ann said, her eyes wide. 'It sounds just lovely. Why did you leave France?'

'Because of cheese,' said Sister Pauline solemnly.

'Cheese?' Ann repeated, confused.

'I was living in the abbey at Saint-Julien-Molin-Molette,' Sister Pauline said, settling down on the garden bench and motioning Ann to join her. 'One day I go out for a walk to buy some cheese. When I return, the other nuns say that they receive news that there is going to be a cultural exchange and I have been chosen to leave the country and join the Assassin Nuns of Pistachio.'

'Like a nun swap?' asked Ann.

'Yes,' replied Sister Pauline. 'That is exactly the right term. A nun swap.'

'Tell me about France,' Ann said. 'I've read so much about it and it always sounds so glamorous and exciting.' She stood up and twirled her skirts around.

'A small town is not so glamorous,' Sister Pauline said, laughing. 'It is very small with not much excitement at all. In the summer, we used to run about in the fields and in the winter, we drink hot chocolate and tell stories around the fire. Sometimes your hair will smell like smoke for many, many days.' She smiled, staring at her feet absently.

'You can't really be afraid of the world like the others over here,' Ann said disbelievingly. 'You sound like you had a lovely time outside.'

'Maybe I was very foolish when I was a child,' Sister Pauline said slowly. 'Maybe I did not understand all the terrible things that can happen. The nuns here, they tell me so many stories of people who have accidents and get hurt and it makes me glad that I live in a safe place.'

'But don't you miss it?' Ann asked. 'Being outside and going places.'

'Ah oui,' Sister Pauline smiled. 'Sometimes I miss it very much.' She looked down at her little guinea pig and stroked the top of his head gently. 'But now I have Bonjour! and I have this abbey and I am happy.'

'I think you'd like Pistachio,' Ann said. 'I think Bonjour! would really like it too. You should come with me sometime and have a little wander.'

'I will think about it,' promised Sister Pauline. 'Now let us start, we have much French to learn today. What do you remember from the lesson we had last week?'

'Aujourd'hui, nous mangeons le tarte-mouffette,' said Ann, carefully pronouncing each word.

'No, no,' Sister Pauline said, giggling uncontrollably. 'What you say means that you are eating a skunk pie. You want to say potato pie, so it is *aujourd'hui, nous mangeons de la tartiflette.*' She stood up and rearranged the skirts of her habit. 'Come, let us go inside and start on some composition.'

The Huberts huddled together on the roof as they watched Ann and Sister Pauline walk across the garden towards the chapel, repeating their French phrases together.

12

'I still can't believe you don't have a bookshop here!' Ann exclaimed one afternoon as she helped Mr Morris add some of Sister Parsnip's onions to the vegetable display outside his shop. The grocer had two large wooden crates propped up at an angle on either side of the entrance to his shop, each lined with straw and filled with neat lines of fresh vegetables. It was an unusually sunny day and Mr Morris was making the most of it by working outside his shop, soaking in the bright sunshine, with the radio on in the background playing old show tunes. A few used cans of paint lay discarded on one side, next to a ladder and some old rags, and the sign above the shop looked shiny and freshly painted.

After standing back to admire her handiwork, Ann readjusted a few orange peppers and put the last onion in its place as Mr Morris added a handwritten sign that read 'Fresh Cheap Veg! Enquire Inside'.

'So what do you do when you finish reading everything you have in your house?' Ann persisted, breathing in the oddly pleasant combination of fresh paint and squashed tomatoes. She had been overly enthusiastic while helping unload the week's produce that morning and there were a few casualties scattered on the ground.

'We're not really allowed books here,' Mr Morris said reluctantly. He stuck a pencil behind his ear and wiped his hands down the sides of his work trousers. 'Right, come along inside and we'll get through your shopping list.' He held the door open for Ann.

'What do you mean, not allowed books?' Ann asked, squinting slightly as her eyes got used to the fluorescent lights inside the shop. 'You mean you're not allowed to read?'

'Oh, we can read,' Mr Morris said. 'As long as it's useful and helps us become more efficient at our work.' He pointed to a large, cloth-bound book next to the till, with the words 'Improving Your Sales Pitch' printed across the spine in dreary silver letters.

'That's not a real book,' Ann scoffed. 'That's just lots and lots of really boring words squashed between two covers. Sister Gwen at the Abbey of Seven Sparrows had a whole collection of equipment manuals that she used to call her library.' She pursed her lips in disapproval. 'She never even read them! Sister Callie said she only kept them to make her look clever.' Mr Morris nodded in agreement as he went over to the till and started to neatly fold the empty sacks and put them in a large crate on the shelf behind him.

'This is a real book,' Ann continued, as she pulled a copy of *Robinson Crusoe* out of her bag and held it out for him to see. Mr Morris's eyes widened and he put down the sack he was folding. '*Robinson Crusoe*!' he exclaimed. 'I remember reading that when I was a boy.' He reached a hand out to touch it, then pulled away quickly. 'You should put that away,' he said, picking the sack up again and refusing to meet Ann's eye. 'There's no room for that here any more.'

'Of course there is,' Ann said as she put the book down on the counter and moved it along towards Mr Morris. 'You should definitely read this instead of that awful looking thing you have there.'

At that very moment, a car pulled up outside the shop and Mr Morris suddenly looked more alert. 'Quick,' he whispered out of the corner of his mouth as he flipped a switch, turning the radio off. 'Take that book and get behind the sack of onions quickly. Don't say anything and don't let him see you.' Ann grabbed her copy of *Robinson Crusoe* and dropped down behind the sacks of supplies just as the bell over the shop door jangled as it opened. Sticking a foot out, she pulled her bag to safety before it could be spotted.

'Hello, Mr Morris,' a deep, syrupy voice said. 'How is business treating you this week?' Ann held her breath and listened intently, trying very hard not to move.

'Just fine, Mr Knight,' the grocer replied, his voice flat and unemotional. When Ann craned her neck around the potatoes, she could see his hands balled up into fists behind the counter.

'Fine is not good enough, Mr Morris,' the man in the shop gave an unpleasant laugh. 'Fine is not really what we're trying to achieve here in Pistachio, is it?'

'Stock's been going quickly,' Mr Morris said evenly. 'Sales are good. I've had to add an extra run on Tuesdays to drop some veg off at the market by the sea as well.'

'New business?' Mr Knight sounded surprised. 'I hope you've registered this with the mayor's office, Mr Morris. You know that you need to pay a higher tax if you're doing more business.'

'It's not really new business,' Mr Morris said quickly. 'I have some extra produce now, so I've been trying—'

'Extra produce!' Mr Knight said suspiciously. 'Where's all this extra produce coming from, may I ask?'

'The nuns from Pistachio have started trading with us again,' Mr Morris replied. 'They grow some excellent vegetables up at the abbey and they've started sending some over in exchange for goods.'

'You mean those stay-at-home nuns who are too afraid to leave the mountain?' Mr Knight laughed again. 'Make sure you're making a profit out of your business with them.'

'I'm doing my job just fine, Mr Knight,' said Mr Morris. 'No complaints from anyone.' As Ann watched, his left leg started to twitch.

'I do hope it stays that way,' Mr Knight said smoothly. 'I wouldn't want to close this little shop down for not complying with regulations, would I?' Ann heard him pick something up from one of the shelves and put it on the counter. 'I'll have a bag of these peanuts,' he said. 'You don't expect me to pay, do you?' Ann watched Mr Morris's hands head up towards the till, then drop down quickly.

'Of course not, Mr Knight,' he mumbled. 'Take what you like from the shop.'

'That's very kind of you,' Mr Knight said unpleasantly. 'If you insist, I'll also take some bread and a box of truffles.' Ann heard the door being shut firmly, and a few seconds later, the car started up again.

'You can come out now,' Mr Morris sounded deflated. 'He won't be back until next week.'

Ann stood up, dusting her dress with her hands. Her knees were covered with streaks of powdered chalk and she had half a cabbage leaf in her hair. 'Who was that?' she asked.

'That was Mr Knight,' the grocer sighed. 'He's the new mayor and the head of the Pistachio Town Committee.' Mr Morris stepped out from behind the counter and rearranged the loaves of bread on the shelf. 'He's not a big fan of new people in the village,' he added. 'I thought I'd save you the trouble of being introduced.'

'Does he just take things without paying for them?' Ann asked. 'And he's the mayor? That doesn't sound very mayor-like to me.'

'Sometimes,' Mr Morris replied, shrugging. 'I find it easier to just let him do what he wants and leave.'

'That sounds an awful lot like bullying,' Ann said, brushing the dust off her dress. 'Sister Felicia at the Parish of Multiple Goats always said that you shouldn't encourage bullies and always stand up for yourself. Can't you tell the police or someone?'

'Mr Knight doesn't answer to the police,' Mr Morris let out a sharp laugh. 'Oh no, Mr Knight doesn't answer to anyone at all.'

'I had a boy like that at the last school I went to,' Ann said thoughtfully. 'So I put a mouse in his desk. It jumped out while he was pulling Ellie Henderson's pigtails and he screamed and screamed until someone took it away.' She smiled proudly, remembering the chaos that resulted. 'That's probably not what Sister Felicia meant for me to do though,' she admitted. 'But he never called me names again.'

'I'm afraid putting a mouse in Mr Knight's car wouldn't really help matters in Pistachio,' Mr Morris said with a twinkle in his eye. 'Although it would make me feel much better!'

'Why did I have to hide the book from him?' Ann asked finally. 'Is he the person who doesn't let people read?' She paused, her eyes wide. 'Is that why you don't have a library?'

'Mr Knight doesn't like us to waste our time on frivolities,' Mr Morris said, shaking his head. 'He says our time is best spent working with no distractions.'

'What happens if you do waste your time on frivolities?' Ann asked, rolling the words around her tongue. She quite liked the word 'frivolities' and decided that she was going to try and use it as much as she could.

Mr Morris took a deep breath. 'Never mind all that, my dear,' he said. 'Let's get your shopping sorted out and fetch some bags for you to carry back to the abbey.' He picked Ann's basket up from behind the counter, where he'd hidden it when Mr Knight had walked in, and started lining up her goods in a neat row by the till.

'Why do you let Mr Knight make all the rules?' Ann persisted. 'Why don't you just tell him that he's being unfair?'

'It doesn't really work like that,' Mr Morris said, putting Ann's shopping into paper bags. 'We've all got families to think about, so it's best not to get the committee upset.'

'That reminds me of something else,' Ann said. 'Just one more question, I promise. Where are all the children?'

Mr Morris shook his head slightly and stared at his hands. 'They're all away at school,' he said. 'They're keeping busy indoors.'

'But it's the weekend and such lovely weather,' Ann said, looking at the bright blue skies outside. 'It seems like such a shame to waste it inside.' The bell over the front door jangled again and Ann froze. Turning around and expecting to see the faceless Mr Knight, she found herself facing a short, plump woman wearing a bright flowered apron instead.

'Oh, hello there!' the woman said excitedly. 'You must be the little one from the abbey I've heard so much about.' She stretched out her arms and enveloped Ann in a warm hug. 'Let's look at you properly,' she said, leaning back and regarding her appraisingly.

'Hello!' Ann said, somewhat startled by the unexpected hug. 'Yes, I'm Ann from the abbey. It's very nice to meet you.'

'Ann, this is my lovely wife,' Mr Morris said, walking over to give her a peck on the cheek. 'She has a lot of questions about the nuns, don't you, my love?'

Mrs Morris was still giving Ann the once-over. 'That's a good head of hair you have there,' she said approvingly. 'Just like my grandmother, and she lived to be a hundred and never stopped talking.' She turned to her husband and sighed. 'I saw that man leave,' she said. 'What did he want this time?'

'Oh, just the usual,' Mr Morris said, wiping the counter down with a duster. 'He wanted to know how business was going and said I need to pay more tax for the new market deliveries.'

'He also took things without paying for them,' Ann piped in indignantly. 'That's practically stealing.'

'Aye, he does that,' Mrs Morris sniffed. 'Takes whatever he wants from everyone.' She turned to her husband. 'He knows we can't afford to pay more taxes,' she said. 'These new rules change every day and I can't keep up with them any more!'

'I had to get Ann to hide in the corner when he came in,' Mr Morris added. 'You know what he's like with new people.' He finished putting the last piece of shopping into the bags and put them down on the ground in front of Ann.

'One more thing,' Ann said, running to the back of the shop as Mr Morris and his wife continued to chat. She returned with a small brown bottle. 'Some Worcestershire sauce for Sister Agnes,' she explained, dropping a few coins on the counter and popping the bottle into her bag.

'Well, at least he didn't walk in on you reading,' Mrs Morris said to her husband. Mr Morris tried to catch her eye, but she didn't notice and continued talking. 'The last time he stopped by the tailoring shop, I was halfway through an exciting part of this week's book and almost didn't put it away in time!'

'I thought you didn't read real books in Pistachio any more!' Ann exclaimed.

Mr and Mrs Morris exchanged uncomfortable glances. 'Oh, I really shouldn't say anything,' Mrs Morris started. She looked at her husband again and shrugged her shoulders. 'She won't tell, will she? He'd be so angry if he found out.'

'Mr Knight?' Ann's eyes were almost as large as saucers. 'You're hiding something from Mr Knight?'

'Of course we're not,' Mr Morris said quickly. 'We're doing nothing illegal. It's just some harmless evening activities.' He shot a quick look outside. 'It's nothing illegal at all,' he repeated, reaching for his keys.

'Are you a superhero with a secret identity?' Ann asked eagerly. 'Are you secretly planning to get rid of that nasty Mr Knight?'

'Oh no, it's nothing that exciting,' Mrs Morris said sheepishly. 'It's just a book club. A few of us get together every week to read and talk about how things used to be.'

'A book club!' Ann squealed, completely blown away by this delightful piece of information. 'I've always wanted to be part of a book club! What are you reading? Please can I come? Where is it?' She stopped to catch her breath. 'You're not reading anything too old for me, are you? I'm not allowed anything very scary or I have trouble sleeping afterwards.' She looked eagerly at both of them. 'This is just wonderful! I've always wanted to be a part of something like this. Please let me join!'

'I don't know if that's a good idea,' Mr Morris said reluctantly. 'I don't really want to get you in any trouble.' He leaned over behind the counter and started to turn off the lights at the far end of shop.

'I don't mind getting into trouble!' Ann insisted. 'Besides, I don't live in the town, so no one's told me to follow any rules here.' She picked her rucksack up and swung it over her shoulders.

'Should we?' Mrs Morris looked at her husband questioningly. 'It would be nice having another face at the meetings. Especially a young one—we do miss having the children here! Everyone else in this town is too afraid of Mr Knight to come join us.'

'I won't tell a soul,' Ann promised. 'And I'll bring brownies and potato fritters and whatever else I can fit into my bag.'

'Oh, I do like brownies,' Mr Morris said, patting his belly. 'We haven't had any nice treats since they shut the local bakery down.'

'So can I come?' Ann asked again, rocking back and forth on her shoes. 'Please?'

'Mr Morris and his wife exchanged glances again. 'I suppose it wouldn't hurt,' Mrs Morris said finally. 'We could all do with a cheery spirit like you around.'

'Yay!' Ann said happily. 'When's the next meeting?'

'In fifteen minutes!' Mr Morris said abruptly, looking at his watch. 'Hurry, hurry! If you leave your bags of shopping here, Ann, I'll lock up and you can pick them up on your way home.' He turned the rest of the lights out, grabbed a set of keys from a nail on the wall, and ushered the other two out of the door and into the empty streets of Pistachio.

13

Ann followed Mr and Mrs Morris down the winding roads that ran through the town of Pistachio. Every so often, one of them stopped, signalling the other to be quiet as they listened carefully for any sounds of an unwanted shadow. Ann was almost beside herself with anticipation. Before she moved to the abbey above Pistachio, the height of excitement had been when Sister Elsie from the Order of Wispy Pines dug up what she thought was an alien fossil in the back garden. On closer inspection it turned out to be a Christmas ornament that had seen better days.

They finally arrived at a long brown building. A cloth banner with the words 'Pistachio's Instant Noodle Factory' was draped over a large rock by the side of it.

'That doesn't look very professional,' Ann pointed out.

'Go take a look at what's under that sign,' Mrs Morris whispered.

Ann crept forward and lifted the cloth up, gasping aloud at what she read underneath. Laid into the rock was a large metal plaque that read 'Pistachio Local Library'. With her eyes now as large as saucers, Ann turned around, overflowing with questions. 'You *do* have a library in Pistachio!' she exclaimed. 'Why is it hidden? Did Mr Knight do this? Where are all the books?'

'Not so loud,' Mrs Morris said, reaching for Ann's hand. 'Through this way, hurry up.' They cut through a small gap in the hedge that surrounded the former library and followed a narrow path that twisted around to the back of the building.

The place looked deserted except for a tiny shaft of yellow light that spilled through the blinds of the window next to the back door. Mr Morris stopped in front of the door and scratched his head. 'I always forget this,' he whispered to Ann. 'Last week, Mrs Allsop opened the door and nearly hit me over the head with a dictionary because I got the knock wrong and they thought I was a spy.' He reached out and tentatively knocked three times and then paused before a fourth knock. The door opened and he ducked inside immediately.

'Evening, my lovelies,' came a cheerful voice and Ann stepped forward to see a rosy-cheeked woman with short curly hair open the door wider to let them in.

'That's not one of our usuals,' she said, staring pointedly at the young girl.

'This is Ann,' Mrs Morris said, putting her arm around Ann's shoulders. 'She's been helping us at the shop.' They stepped in through the door and into the building together. 'She's from the abbey,' Mrs Morris continued. 'Ann's been bringing some lovely vegetables from the nuns to trade with us every week.'

'I didn't think the nuns came down to Pistachio any more,' the woman said. She locked the door behind them and turned the lights up as Ann looked around with interest.

It was a long room with large cardboard boxes stamped with 'Pistachio's Instant Noodles' and 'PIN' piled high against the walls. As Ann glanced around, she could tell it was once a library. There were stained, rectangular patches on the wall where pictures had once hung and a few empty card organizers lay piled by the side of some boxes. Further in the corner, there were several wooden shelves lined up against one side of the room, filled with broken bits of machinery instead of books.

In the middle of the room, however, a small group of people sat in a circle of folding chairs around a table. Mrs Morris drew up a chair and motioned Ann to come and sit by her. 'These are the last few people who like to remember things the way they used to be,' she whispered. 'The others have given up and just do everything Mr Knight tells them to.'

'That's Mr and Mrs Skillet,' Mrs Morris said, pointing at the curly-haired lady who let them in and a bearded man who stood next to her. 'They have a farm just outside Pistachio with the loveliest lambs you've ever seen. Mrs Skillet makes the wonderful jams we have in the shop. She has a magic hand with fruit, I tell you.'

Ann made a mental note to buy some jam for the abbey. She'd been wondering what had been missing from the breakfast table! 'Who's that?' she asked, looking at a large grizzled man in a tweed jacket and a flat cap, who sat next to a tiny woman with long dark hair and a bag of knitting in her lap.

'That's Farmer Argyll and his wife,' Mrs Morris said. 'Mrs Argyll works at the tailoring shop with me and she's a wonder with the needles. She could knit you a sweater in a day if she wanted to.' Mr Morris waved at her from across the room.

'Sorry, I'll be back in a minute,' Mrs Morris said. 'I'll go help get the biscuits and tea out. Balancing a tray without dropping anything is not one of Mr Morris's talents.' Ann watched her bustle across the room to join her husband.

A slightly ditzy-looking woman with flyaway blonde hair wearing a striped dress sat on the chair next to Ann, looking through a box of children's picture books.

'Hello, I'm Mrs Allsop,' she said, waving at Ann, the silver bracelets on her arm tinkling as she moved. 'Mr Allsop couldn't be here because he works the night shift at the mill,' she explained, cocking her head to one side as she looked at a book about elephants.

'My name is Ann,' Ann said, waving back. 'Mr and Mrs Morris brought me here. I'm from the abbey.'

'Oh dear, what's she doing now?' Mrs Allsop reached down under the table to grab hold of a chubby baby who was just in the process of putting her entire shoe into her mouth. 'This is Emmy,' she added. 'Emmy just loves meeting new people, don't you, darling?' She picked her daughter up and fussed over her, pulling faces and cooing into her ear. Emmy ignored her mother's attempts to make her smile and stared at Ann. Ann, who after a lifetime of growing up with various middle-aged nuns, was not used to being around babies and stared right back at her.

'Hello, Emmy,' Ann said politely, shaking the baby's chubby fist. Emmy appreciated being treated with the respect she felt she deserved. Most adults tended to pat her on the head or—on some horrifying occasions—grab her by the cheek. She had a feeling this small adult with enormous hair was a kindred spirit and gurgled at her.

'Is everyone here?' Mr Morris asked, standing up to do a quick headcount as he put a basket of fruit on the table. Mrs Morris carried the tray around the room, making sure everyone had a mug and a treat. 'Has everyone brought a book to read?'

The people around the room each held up a different book. 'This isn't your regular book club,' Mrs Morris explained as she sat down next to Ann with a cup of tea and a paperback novel. 'We just come here every evening so we have a place to read and have a bit of friendly chat.'

'Where are the children?' Ann asked Mrs Allsop as she bit into her biscuit. 'Emmy's the only child I've seen in Pistachio. Where are all the others?'

Mr and Mrs Morris exchanged glances as Mr Skillet coughed violently. 'They've all been sent to a boarding school,' Mrs Skillet said, twisting the hem of her cardigan. 'Mr Knight said that the school here wasn't good enough, and if we really wanted to help our children, we needed to send them away to get a better education.' She looked over at the baby playing on the floor. 'Emmy was too little to go to school, so she's still here.'

'He asks about her all the time though,' Mrs Allsop said, frowning. 'Always checking how old she is and whether she's learning to talk yet. He's trying to get rid of her as soon as possible.'

'He thinks we'd be more productive if we weren't distracted by what he calls frivolities and nonsense,' Mrs Skillet scoffed. 'No more children playing outside, no more festival days, no more cafes or restaurants, no more Cheesecake Fridays at the local bakery, no more . . . fun,' she sighed.

'He's even got a factory where he pulps books,' Mrs Argyll added quietly, as Ann looked horrified. 'We tried to rescue as many as we could, but he got to most of Pistachio's collection.'

'At first we thought it was a joke,' Mr Morris said. 'It didn't seem possible that anyone would want to live a life that gloomy. We were certain that the deputy mayor would tell him that his demands were impossible and that it wasn't going to happen.' He helped himself to an apple from the fruit bowl and took a large bite out of it. 'But maybe Mr Smythe was blinded by the possibility of the town becoming a big success, or maybe he really believed we weren't doing much with our businesses. Anyway, Mr Knight now runs everything in the town, and no one's seen very much of Mr Smythe ever since.'

'How does Mr Knight own everything?' Ann asked. 'Haven't you lived here for years?'

'Because of your nuns,' Mrs Skillet said, shaking her head as she took a sip of tea.

'The Assassin Nuns are the protectors of any town that they live near,' explained Mr Skillet, his bushy eyebrows twitching as he spoke. 'The old nuns used to always make sure that things were going well down here in Pistachio. We never even needed a mayor. We've only had a deputy for years. But over the last fifteen years or so, they haven't left the mountain.'

'There's paperwork to be filled out every so often,' added Mrs Morris. 'The nuns haven't signed anything for years, so Mr Knight took the opportunity to swoop in and convince the deputy mayor that he should be in charge.' She shook her head sadly. 'He got them to make him the mayor instead.'

'Now he says that if we don't listen to him, he'll evict us from our homes because he owns them now.'

'That's just terrible!' Ann said. 'Can he really do that? It sounds illegal.' Emmy sat up and tossed half a biscuit at her mother in agreement.

'There's no one really to stop him,' Mrs Skillet said. 'Because we used to have the Assassin Nuns to protect us back in the day, we don't have a local police force here. There's no one to arrest him and no one to report him to.'

'I'm going to tell the nuns,' Ann announced, standing up. 'If they knew that they're supposed to come down here and take over as actual guardians of the town, I'm sure they'll leave the abbey right away and make things right!'

'I wouldn't be so sure,' Mrs Skillet said dryly. 'We send them a reminder to come sign the town charter every year during the Summer and Winter Festivals. They never reply and they never come.'

'I'm sure they don't know,' Ann insisted. 'I know them. They're lovely people and would want to help if they knew that the town was really in trouble.'

'I haven't seen them for years now,' Farmer Argyll said. 'The ones we had back then were champion Assassin Nuns! Always on the lookout for trouble and happy to help with anything. This lot don't really bother with us any more.'

'I'm telling them right away,' Ann said, grabbing her things and heading for the door.

'Hold up,' Mr Morris said, putting his tea down and reaching for his keys. 'I'll walk you to the shop so you can get your things. I'll give you a torch, too,' he added. 'It gets dark quickly this time of year.'

Later, as Ann raced up the mountain, eager to tell the nuns that there was a reason for them to leave their beloved abbey, Mrs Skillet and Mrs Allsop tidied away the empty plates and glasses in the old library. Emmy was fast asleep in the corner, two chairs and Mrs Allsop's coat serving as a temporary bed.

'Do you think she'll be able to get them to come down here?' Mrs Allsop asked.

'Ah, I doubt it,' Mrs Skillet said. 'Even if she does, what are a bunch of old nuns going to do to stop Mr Knight and his men?'

'That's true,' Mrs Allsop agreed, putting the empty cups into a big bag to take home.

'That's probably the last we've seen of that girl as well,' Mrs Skillet remarked as she put her book into her bag and started turning the lights off. 'Once she tells them she wants to get involved, they'll probably talk her out of coming back here again.'

'Pity,' Mrs Allsop said, slinging her bag across her shoulder and picking the still sleeping Emmy up carefully. 'It was nice having a child around here again.' She peeked through the blinds before she opened the door to make sure no one was outside spying on them, and both women disappeared into the night.

14

The record player was on and the abbey was filled with the strains of classical music when Ann burst into the living room and dropped her bags of shopping on the floor. 'I've found out what's happening in Pistachio!' she exclaimed. The nuns were sitting in their usual spots around the living room, while the Reverend Mother sat at the desk, writing letters.

'Hello, Ann,' Sister Pauline called out from the armchair in front of the fireplace. Bonjour! was curled up in the crook of her arm, fast asleep. 'What is happening?'

'You're late,' Sister Beatrice said, looking pointedly at the clock. 'Terribly late.' She pushed her glasses up her nose and stared at Ann gravely.

'I was so worried,' Sister Ruth said, looking at Ann with relief. 'I thought something terrible had happened to you.' She got up and headed towards the kitchen. 'I'll get you some chickpea stew,' she said. 'It's been sitting in the oven so it's still nice and warm. Maybe some bread on the side with some butter.'

'Wait,' Ann said. 'I've got something to tell you.' She started to unbutton her coat and unwrap her scarf hurriedly. 'We have to do something,' she said earnestly. 'You have to help me. It's the town.'

Sister Sparkplug was polishing her spanners with an old piece of stained flannel, staring at them through her round motorcycle glasses, while Vroom lay peacefully folded up by the fire. 'What's happened to Pistachio?' she asked, rubbing a particularly stubborn spot of grease.

'There's a man running the town,' Ann said, her words jumbling together as she tried to get them all out at once. 'It's the new mayor and his name is Mr Knight. He got there only last year and he's changed everything. He's terrible! He won't let people read or have fun and now he owns the whole town and they can't make him leave because if they do, he'll take away all their homes!' She stopped to take a breath, her face still furrowed with a frown. 'He's sent all the children away to boarding school,' she continued. 'And he turns books into pulp in his factories. He destroys books!'

'So that's what all that smoke is on the far side of town,' Sister Ruth said, turning to Sister Sparkplug. 'I did wonder about that.' Sister Sparkplug nodded, examining her spanners carefully in the firelight.

'That sounds very unpleasant,' Sister Agnes agreed. 'They should really do something about it.' She yawned widely and looked at the clock. 'Almost bedtime for me, I'm afraid,' she said, standing up and reaching for her glasses. 'I'm glad you're back safe, Ann, but please try to get home earlier next time. Goodnight, everyone. I'll see you at morning prayers.'

'But . . . aren't you going to do something about it?' Ann asked, shocked at their lack of interest.

'Who, me?' Sister Agnes looked puzzled. 'What would I do?'

'Not just you, all of you,' Ann said, looking around the room. 'I thought all of you could come down to the town with me and set things right.'

'Set things right?' Sister Ruth chuckled. 'Us?'

'Yes,' Ann said. 'I thought you could help them.' She looked over at the pictures on the wall. 'Like the old Assassin Nuns,' she continued, running her fingers through her hair in frustration. 'They used to help the town all the time, I've heard all about it. I thought you would, too.'

'We haven't been off this mountain in years,' Sister Sparkplug said, shaking her head ruefully. 'We wouldn't know the first thing about helping anyone, much less getting rid of some sort of nasty character.' She put the last of her tools away and pushed her glasses up onto her head. 'Why would you want us to go there?'

'But you're the Assassin Nuns!' Ann exclaimed, tugging at her dress impatiently. 'Isn't that what you do? Aren't you supposed to help people?'

'Well, if someone showed up at our doorstep with a flat type or a broken leg, of course we would let them in and help them,' Sister Ruth said, taking a sip of cocoa. 'Of course we would.'

'As soon as we determined that they didn't have any sort of infectious disease or a hidden weapon,' interrupted Sister Beatrice.

'But why would we go out there and actually look for trouble?' Sister Ruth continued serenely. 'That seems like a very silly thing to do.'

'It is true,' Sister Pauline said. 'I do not think it is the good idea to go running into a place where there is a problem.'

'But you're the Assassin Nuns of Pistachio!' Ann said. 'They told me that you're the ones meant to protect them. That's what it says in the town charter! If you don't go down there, Mr Knight will never leave!'

'I'm sure everything's fine,' Sister Agnes said again. 'If they really were in trouble, they would alert the police or the army or something.'

'I'm alerting you!' Ann said. 'You had an agreement with the town to watch over them—they told me! All you have to do is come back there with me and get rid of Mr Knight.'

'Are they still harping on about that town charter?' the Reverend Mother asked, shaking her head. 'Every single year, they send us that reminder to sign the thing. What on earth do they want us to do? We have nothing to do with that town any more. The old nuns got rid of all their problems.'

'We're hardly the best people to have around in a crisis, anyway,' Sister Parsnip agreed. 'I can deal with weeds, not evil villains.'

'I can't believe you don't want to help,' Ann said slowly. 'They told me you wouldn't listen, but I didn't believe them. I didn't think you could be so horrible!'

'Now that's a little unfair,' said Sister Ruth. 'We live here, in the abbey. We deal with our own problems. I'm sure the people of Pistachio can deal with their own problems as well.'

'Maybe that Mr Knight isn't so bad,' Sister Agnes suggested. 'Maybe the townspeople just had a bad day and were doing a spot of complaining. I get like that sometimes.'

'That's true,' Sister Sparkplug said. 'When I first came to live here, I thought Sister Ruth was simply awful. Then I realized that she just gets grumpy when she's hungry.'

'Yes, it's probably just a mix-up,' Sister Parsnip said. 'I'm sure there's no real reason to go down to Pistachio to investigate anything.'

'It's all a lie,' Ann said accusingly. 'Everyone thinks you're brave and wonderful. When I was at all those other abbeys, I used to hear them talk about the wonderful things the Assassin Nuns did.'

'It's not our fault that people think we're still assassins,' Sister Agnes said defensively, looking at the Reverend Mother. 'That's what the old nuns were like. And, besides, the town seems fine. There can't be that much wrong with it.'

'It still looks like it always has,' Sister Parsnip agreed. 'I haven't noticed anything different when I'm out in the garden and looking down at the valley. It's just as peaceful as always.'

'Of course it looks the same from up here!' Ann said, exasperated. 'It's what's happening down there that's the problem!'

'We're not really qualified to deal with any problems a town might have,' started the Reverend Mother. 'This sort of issue is best dealt with by—'

'But you're the Assassin Nuns!' Ann interrupted. She stood up and looked at each of them, not understanding why they insisted on being so stubborn. 'You're supposed to protect that town! That's why you're here. That's why they built this stupid abbey in the first place!'

The nuns took a sharp breath in unison. Sister Mildew looked confused and rummaged about for her ear trumpet. 'What's that she said?' she asked, holding it up to her ear.

'She called the abbey stupid,' whispered Sister Parsnip, her eyes wide. 'No one's ever called the abbey stupid before.'

'Not to our faces anyway,' Sister Beatrice added dryly.

'Sister Pauline?' Ann looked at the French nun beseechingly.

'I'm sorry, *ma cherie*,' Sister Pauline shook her head and looked away. 'I cannot help you with this.' Bonjour! woke up and stared apologetically at Ann from her pocket, his beady eyes bright in the firelight.

'Now, I understand why you're upset,' the Reverend Mother said, standing up. 'You got to know these people and you want to help them.' She paused and looked at the other nuns before continuing. 'I understand that, but we really can't help.'

Ann stared at her uncomprehendingly. 'Why not?' she asked.

'We're not like the old nuns,' the Reverend Mother said evenly. 'Those were different times and they were braver women. If it makes you feel any better, we'll say a special prayer for them tomorrow. We can help that way.'

'But you'd be so much more of a help if you just went there!' Ann cried. 'You have to get involved!'

'We did try to get involved!' the Reverend Mother said. 'We asked for a senior nun to help us figure out whether there was something going on.' She exchanged a quick glance with Sister Agnes, who shook her head furiously in agreement. 'We did ask for help,' the Reverend Mother continued. 'But then you arrived instead and the town seems fine now.'

'So you never asked for me,' Ann said, her eyes bright with tears. 'I thought you wanted me here.'

'There must have been a pigeon-related error,' Sister Parsnip said quickly. 'Something got mixed up somewhere.'

'Were you going to send me back?' Ann asked, her voice quiet.

'We decided not to!' Sister Ruth exclaimed. 'We decided that we needed you in the abbey after all.'

'You never wanted me and now you won't help me,' Ann said. She grabbed her scarf and coat as she ran from the room, her eyes brimming with tears. The nuns sat in the awkward silence that followed, as the Reverend Mother stood staring at the door.

'I knew this would happen,' Sister Beatrice said. 'I just knew it.' She got up and used a poker to readjust the logs, sending a tiny shower of sparks up the chimney. 'I knew this would happen the minute we let a child into the abbey.'

'I'm sure the town is fine,' Sister Agnes repeated for the third time that evening, but no one was really listening to her any more.

15

The next day, Ann ignored Sister's Ruth's call for breakfast and remained in bed. She ignored the knocks on her door and pretended to be asleep when they stuck their heads in to see if she was alright. She even kept her eyes tightly shut when Sister Pauline brought Bonjour! in to see her and he ran across her shoulder and sniffed at her face.

'She won't talk,' Sister Agnes said to the Reverend Mother as they both stood in the doorway staring at Ann as she lay in bed, her back to them. 'She won't get out of bed either.'

The Reverend Mother sighed. She didn't have much experience dealing with children and she wasn't sure whether Ann was really ill or just cross with them for not helping the people of Pistachio. 'Let's leave her be for a bit,' she said finally.

'Maybe she's just tired and needs some rest. All that walking up and down the mountain must be quite exhausting.'

'I'll ask Sister Ruth to bring her some food,' Sister Agnes said. 'The girl needs to eat, even if she's tired.' The nuns closed the door and walked down the corridor, their voices fading away.

Ann could hear Sister Beatrice in the garden, talking to the pigeons, and Sister Parsnip happily humming as she wandering around in her vegetable plot. She scowled and pulled her pillow around her ears, trying to drown out all the sounds of the abbey.

In a few minutes there was another knock on the door and Sister Ruth came in carrying a plate of sandwiches and a glass of milk. 'Hello there,' she called out. Ann buried her head further into her duvet and didn't answer.

'Well, I hope you feel better soon,' Sister Ruth continued. 'The Reverend Mother says you might be a bit poorly so I made you some ham sandwiches for a late lunch. Nothing too fancy.' Ann stuck an eye out and looked at the plate, her stomach starting to rumble ever so slightly. 'Well, I'll just leave these here,' Sister Ruth said. 'I'll be down in the kitchen if you need anything.'

Ann waited until she'd left and wolfed the sandwiches down, realizing that she hadn't eaten all day. She looked out of the window as she slowly drank her milk and watched the nuns go about doing their various chores—feeding the chickens, picking fruit and hanging laundry out to dry. She wiped her milk moustache off with the back of her hand and glowered at them. It made her incredibly angry to think that they were perfectly happy living their little lives up on the mountain while the town they were supposed to protect was in trouble. She got back into bed and pulled the covers over her head, trying to decide what to do.

Ann woke up with a start to realize that she had slept through most of the afternoon. A quick look at the clock told her that it had been a few hours since she nodded off and it was almost time for bed again. Her empty plate and glass were gone and there was a note propped up on her bedside table. 'There are some bits and pieces in the kitchen for you to eat', it read, each word slanting in Sister Ruth's familiar handwriting. 'Didn't want to wake you, so help yourself when you're up and hungry.'

Ann got out of bed quickly and changed into a clean dress and cardigan. Reaching for a pen, she turned Sister Ruth's note over and added her own message to it. 'In case you come in to check on me, I'm going to Pistachio for a meeting. Some of the people gather together in the evenings and they're brave, so I want to help them. I'll be back soon, don't bother worrying.' Ann read it again and decided it would do. She propped it carefully on her pillow, grabbed her bag and Mr Morris's torch, and left the room.

***

Making her way down the streets of Pistachio as the sun dipped behind the mountains, Ann was still angry at the nuns for not wanting to help the townspeople. As a matter of fact, the last time she had been this angry at a group of nuns was when the Sisters of Painful Solitude had given all her books away because they thought she was being distracted by the charms of the world. It had taken Ann almost a year to get her collection together again.

As she walked past Old Joel's shop, she could see Zeus in his cage though the window. 'Hair!' he squawked, staring at her with beady eyes and shuffling along his perch. 'Hair! Hair! Hair!'

'Shhh!' she said, holding her finger to her lips. 'Go to sleep, you silly bird!'

'Sleep!' Zeus screamed, as Ann walked away from him as fast as she could. 'Hair! Sleep! Sleep!'

With the hysterical parrot behind her, Ann evened out her pace and kept an eye out on the empty streets as she walked through them. She stayed in the shadows, trying to remember the route Mr and Mrs Morris had taken the previous day to get to the old library.

There was a narrow strip of light filtering though the blinds of the window at the back of the building when she finally got there. She knocked three times, like she remembered Mr Morris doing, then paused and knocked again. The door opened a crack and Mrs Argyll peered out, squinting at Ann. 'Oh, it's you,' she sounded surprised. 'Come on in.' Mrs Argyll checked both sides of the road to make sure Ann hadn't been followed and then closed the door firmly.

The room was filled with the same people Ann remembered from the last meeting. Farmer Argyll tipped his flat cap at her, while Mrs Skillet and her husband smiled as they passed around plastic cups full of punch. Mrs Allsop and Emmy sat in the far corner of the room, looking at a picture book together. The lights had been turned down low, and there was a set of candles in ornate holders on the table in the middle, with drops of wax spilling onto the oilcloth that covered it.

'I didn't think you'd be back so soon,' Mrs Morris whispered to Ann as she ushered her to her seat. 'Aren't you supposed to come down to the town just once a week?'

'I don't want to live at the abbey any more,' Ann said sullenly. 'They're just a bunch of cowards hiding in an abbey on top of the mountain.' She sat down on a folding chair next to a pile of cardboard boxes that smelled faintly of stale noodles. 'I hate them.'

'Oh, don't you say that,' Mrs Morris said, shaking her head. 'You were so happy there the last time we talked. I'm sure they have a very good reason for staying up on the mountain.'

'No, they don't!' Ann exclaimed. 'They're just afraid of every single thing in the world for no reason at all and don't want me to get involved either.'

'So they don't know you're here?' Mrs Morris looked concerned. 'Oh dear. They're going to be very worried when they notice that you're missing.' She tried to catch Mr Morris's eye from across the room. 'Maybe we should walk you back to the abbey now so that everything gets sorted.'

'No, I'll be back before they wake up,' Ann said, rummaging through her bag. 'They won't even know I was away.'

'If you're sure,' Mrs Morris said uncertainly. Her eyes lit up when Ann pulled a paper bag of scones and a cold ham out of her rucksack. 'Why, what do we have here?'

'It's for the meeting,' Ann said. 'I thought people might like some snacks.' She buried her arm in her bag again and pulled out a loaf of bread and a small glass bottle. 'Fresh rye for ham sandwiches and some of Sister Ruth's elderflower cordial,' she said, handing the items over to the increasingly more delighted Mrs Morris.

'This is excellent,' Mrs Morris said. 'We haven't had a party tea since before the town changed. This is bound to lift spirits!' She tidied some space on the table and laid the food out, digging through a box on the floor for the miniature plastic cutlery that often accompanied packs of instant noodles.

'What's a party tea?' Ann asked, already deciding that she liked the sound of it very much.

'Oh, it's just a selection of lots of little bits of nice fancy food,' Mrs Morris replied, bustling around the table and arranging paper plates. 'Vol-au-vents and little pastries and whatnot. My mother always did one for birthdays and other celebrations.' She smiled reminiscently. 'You could pile your plate high with all these wonderful different things. It really was most delightful.'

'Is that a party tea I see there?' Mrs Allsop and Emmy arrived to investigate. 'Oh, look at that! Isn't that just lovely, Emmy?' Emmy tried to wriggle out of her mother's grip and capture the large tempting ham in the middle of the table, but was immediately whisked away to a safe distance, much to her disappointment.

Ann wandered over to say hello to the others, who were having a heated discussion over plastic cups of punch. 'He can't keep us prisoner in our own town,' Mr Skillet said. 'The only reason he's getting away with this is because no one's standing up to him.'

Mrs Argyll nodded in agreement. 'If we can just get people to realize that there's no need to be afraid of that man, he'll soon be gone and we can go back to the way things used to be.'

'Do you remember the old Summer and Winter Festival weekends?' Mrs Skillet asked. 'They seem like so long ago now.'

'Aye,' Farmer Argyll smiled. 'I had the finest pig in the county, Horace. He won a ribbon at the last festival we had.' Farmer Argyll paused and scratched his head. 'That was the day Mr Knight first showed up, come to think of it. Drove up in that shiny black car of his and made us stop doing everything we loved.'

'The next day the deputy mayor called us all to the town hall for a meeting,' Mr Morris said to Ann with a sigh. 'He said things were going to change in Pistachio and that we'd been wasting our time with pointless things like the annual festivals. He said he'd been discussing matters with Mr Knight and they'd both decided that it was in the town's best interests that full control of the Pistachio Town Committee should be given to Mr Knight and that he was now our new mayor.'

'Then that terrible man took the microphone and told us that he was closing down all the places he thought were distracting us from performing to our full potential,' Mrs Skillet said, sniffing with disgust. 'And all this happened.'

'I miss those days,' Mrs Allsop said sadly, sitting down next to them. 'It was lovely before he sent the children away to boarding school.' She put the picture book back in the box under her chair. 'Some evenings we'd go watch the boys fly their kites over the common, wouldn't we, Emmy?' Emmy, however, had no interest whatsoever in her mother's rambling stories and was still trying to find a way to escape and investigate that enormous, potentially delicious object she'd been separated from.

'They don't talk about much when they do write,' Mr Morris said gruffly. 'Letters every weekend and they seem to be busy with far too much schoolwork than they ought to.'

'There aren't enough of us here to make a difference,' Mrs Argyll said quietly, her hands folded neatly in her lap. 'It's going to take more than the handful of people in this room to bring someone like Mr Knight down.'

'Let's get more of the townspeople involved in the book club,' Mrs Skillet suggested, leaning forward earnestly. 'When they see that it's okay to have a bit of fun, they might realize that Mr Knight doesn't have all the answers and it's time we took the town back from him.'

'That's a brilliant idea,' Mr Morris said, standing up and rubbing his hands together happily. 'Now let's settle down and have this party tea that's been waiting.'

In the excitement that ensued, no one heard a car pulling up outside, and the sound of measured steps on the cobbled path leading to the back of the building were all but missed. Only Emmy paused and peered suspiciously at the gap in the blinds, her baby sense telling her something was terribly wrong, but Mrs Allsop gave her a piece of scone to taste, and she looked away from the window just as Mr Knight's cold, angular face appeared there.

16

There was a loud knock on the door, interrupting the cheerful talk at the table as Mrs Morris made the sandwiches and passed them on to the others. Mr Skillet, who had just taken a large sip of cordial, sat up in surprise and began to cough uncontrollably. As Mr Morris and Farmer Argyll exchanged panicked glances, Ann had a sudden feeling of cold dread creep up her spine. 'There's no one else left to come tonight, is there?' Mrs Allsop whispered to Mrs Argyll as she quickly scanned the room. 'You didn't manage to talk any of the others into showing up, did you?' Mrs Argyll shook her head.

There was another knock on the door—louder and more insistent. Mrs Skillet jumped up and motioned to the others to hide the books. 'Who is it?' she asked, her voice surprisingly calm. 'I'm just doing some after-hours cleaning here, that's all.' Farmer Argyll stood up, twisting his cap nervously.

There was a loud crash as a piece of wood broke through the windowpane, scattering shards of glass over the wooden floor. Mrs Skillet jumped, knocking over a pile of empty boxes, while Mr Morris reached out to grab hold of Mrs Morris's hand. 'Who's there?' Mrs Skillet repeated, backing into the room. A pair of large hands appeared through the gaping hole and grabbed the latch, turning it menacingly as the window was jerked up and the blinds ripped down.

There was silence for a few seconds, and then a man's face appeared at the window, an unpleasant smile tugging at his sallow cheeks. His dark hair was slicked back and a large black bowtie sat incongruously on his neck. Ann felt her breath catch in her throat as she realized this was her first clear look at the infamous Mr Knight. 'What's all this?' he spoke in the smooth, oily tones she remembered from when she was hiding in Mr Morris's shop. 'Are we planning something illegal here?' He snapped his fingers and three large men in black overcoats broke in through the door. 'Search the room,' he said to them, disappearing back into the darkness.

The men kicked down the piles of boxes and dug through the papers on the floor as the members of the book club gathered together in the far corner of the room. Ann watched as they knocked the paper plates to the floor, trampling over the sandwiches and scones with their heavy boots. 'We aren't doing anything wrong!' Mrs Allsop cried out, holding Emmy close to her. 'You have no right to barge in and do this to us.'

'I'm afraid that's not true, my dear,' Mr Knight said silkily, as he strolled in through the door. 'I have every

right to do this and you know it. The town charter states that all forms of distracting entertainment are to be banned.' He crouched down, the tails of his jacket trailing the ground, and picked up a book from the pile under the table. 'This is exactly the sort of thing that I mean. Planting unnecessary thoughts in your head and making you think that there's more to life than a job well done.' He stood up, his voice suddenly hard and cold. 'I will not tolerate this.'

'There *is* more to life!' Ann cut in, taking a step towards him. 'There's absolutely nothing wrong with reading a story or having a party tea with some friends at the end of the day.' She stood there, folding her arms and staring up at him defiantly.

'Well, well, well,' Mr Knight said in surprise, leaning down to take a better look at Ann. 'What do we have here? I don't think I've seen you around this town before. What are you doing here?'

'I'm from the abbey on top of the mountain,' Ann replied boldly. 'And the Assassins Nuns know what you're up to.'

'The Assassin Nuns?' Mr Knight said, tilting his head back to laugh. 'Oh, I know all about your precious Assassin Nuns.' He stretched his long fingers out and rested their tips together, smirking at Ann over them. 'They haven't left that abbey in fifteen years. They don't care about this town. Not one tiny bit.'

'That's not true,' Ann said. 'They'll come. You just wait and see.' She watched the men comb the room, tossing papers aside and ripping open cardboard boxes. The candles on the table had been knocked over and melted wax dripped down onto the trampled scones on the floor.

'We're not doing anything wrong,' Mrs Allsop repeated, her face pale as she rocked Emmy back and forth on her shoulder. 'Who told you we were here?'

'Did you think I wouldn't find out about your little meetings?' Mr Knight said scornfully. 'After hours in the old library, reading your stupid books?' He watched as his henchmen collected every last book from the room and piled them on the floor in front of him. 'These are all going to be pulped,' he said with relish. 'Each and every one of these.' The men put them in a box and carried them outside while Mr Knight watched the rest of them, a nasty smile dancing across his face. 'There will be consequences for this, you know,' he said. 'I'm going to make an example of all of you to discourage this sort of behaviour.'

'We're not afraid of you,' Farmer Argyll said, putting his flat cap back on and folding his arms across his chest. 'You don't belong in this town and you have no right to make any of the rules.'

'Of course I do,' Mr Knight said, his voice rising. 'I'm the mayor. This means I'm allowed to do anything to make the town a better place if I think it's necessary.' He looked at the rest of them and smirked. 'And that's what I'm doing right now.'

'There are more of us,' Mrs Morris said, her voice uneven. 'There are plenty of people in this town who don't want you here any more. Even if you stop us, more of them will start standing up to you. You can't just crush an entire town.'

'I do believe I can,' Mr Knight laughed harshly. 'Where are these people now? I don't see them here. I just see you, a handful of your pitiful neighbours and one baby.' He leaned back in his chair, looking at them through heavy, lidded eyes. 'And you're going to pay for this insubordination.'

'Let the girl go back home,' Mrs Skillet said, putting her arm around Ann's shoulders. 'She doesn't even live here so she shouldn't have to be a part of all this.'

'I'm afraid that's not going to happen,' Mr Knight said. 'She's going to come with me.' Mrs Skillet's grip around her shoulder tightened as Ann heard her inhale sharply.

'She's just a child!' Mrs Morris said, stepping forward. One of Mr Knight's henchmen frowned at her threateningly until she joined the others back in the corner.

'Are you afraid I'll tell the Assassin Nuns what you're doing?' Ann asked, scowling at Mr Knight. 'Because they already know. I've left them a note telling them I'm here and if I don't go back home tonight, they'll come down here and you'll be sorry.'

'Let me tell you what I know about the Assassin Nuns,' Mr Knight spoke directly to Ann, his voice sharp and clear. 'I've done my research well.' He sat down on one of the chairs and motioned Ann to come closer. 'They used to be quite formidable once, I'll give them that. They were quite a little band of heroes when the abbey was first built. Always championing for the rights of the people and making sure everyone in the town was happy and safe, fighting crime, shooting intruders and putting away thieves. And then do you know what happened?'

He leaned forward, staring at Ann with those unpleasant eyes. 'They eventually left. The new nuns who came in were completely different. They thought that it was much easier to stay up on top of the mountain where things were safe rather than actually go out and help people. And over the years, that's what they've all told each other.' He laughed scornfully. 'So to answer your question, no, I'm not afraid of the Assassin Nuns. They're never going to leave their precious mountain to help you because they don't care about anyone except themselves.'

As he spoke, Ann felt the first sliver of doubt in her mind. Was she absolutely certain the nuns would come and get her? They hadn't seemed that concerned about the town when she told them about Mr Knight earlier. She shook her head firmly and told herself not to be silly. Of course they would come and rescue her. 'They'll come and get me,' she said again, but this time there was a slight quiver in her voice.

'Take them away,' Mr Knight said to his men, waving at the townspeople. 'Put them somewhere for tonight and we'll deal with them tomorrow.' Emmy started to howl indignantly. She remembered Mr Knight and was certain that his presence meant that something nasty was about to happen.

'You're coming with me,' he said, pointing at Ann. He motioned to one of his bodyguards. 'Put her in the car,' he said. 'We'll be sending her off to boarding school with the others.'

Ann turned around to say goodbye to the others, but Mr Knight's henchmen pushed her out of the room before she would get a word out. She could just make out Emmy's tiny hand waving at her though the broken window as the men shoved her towards the yawning black depths of Mr Knight's car.

17

As they drove through the dark and quiet streets of Pistachio, Mr Knight sat on one side of the back seat looking out of the window, while Ann stared sullenly out of the other. Two of Mr Knight's henchmen sat in the front, their broad shoulders filling up the seat. Ann felt along the side of the door for a handle, but found that the doors were missing any sort of latch on the inside. 'This is kidnapping, you know,' she said, folding her hands and glaring at him. 'You're going to get into so much trouble for doing this.'

'I can assure you this isn't kidnapping,' Mr Knight said, turning towards her with an unpleasant laugh. 'You don't belong in this town, you see, so what you're doing is trespassing. I'm just dealing with an unwanted intruder.'

'I'm not an intruder!' Ann exclaimed. 'No one said I couldn't come here. You're just making this up as you go along.'

'There are rules here,' Mr Knight declared, looking out of the window at the shuttered windows of each house as they passed by. 'People who abide by these rules don't have anything to worry about from me. Troublemakers like you, however, will get what's coming to them.'

'What's going to happen to the others?' Ann asked. 'To Mr Morris and Mrs Allsop and the rest?'

'They're going to be taught a lesson,' Mr Knight said smoothly. 'Perhaps a little accident at the grocer's shop or a small fire at the tailor's. Nothing too devastating, just something to remind them that there are consequences for their actions. As for the farmers, I might take some of their precious animals away.' He straightened his bowtie with a flourish. 'They need to understand that I mean business and I don't like people who make things difficult.'

The road wound out of Pistachio as the car sped away into the darkness. Ann stared out at the unfamiliar terrain as the trees thinned out and the ground stretched out in front of them, rocky and bare. 'I don't want to go to boarding school,' she said in a small voice. 'I need to go back to the abbey.'

'Oh, it's not strictly a boarding school,' Mr Knight said, smiling out at the darkness. 'It's a place where you'll learn a few manners and the importance of hard work.'

The car pulled up outside a large grey building at the side of the road. A thick hedge surrounded it, and there was a big wrought-iron gate in front. A broad-shouldered man in a black jumper stepped out from the shadows—Ann was starting to realize that all of Mr Knight's henchmen looked fairly alike—and opened the gates for them as the car pulled through.

Ann stepped out of the car and looked up at the building in front of her. The windows were barred and shut, giving the place a sinister look and making Ann suddenly homesick for the welcoming sight of the ivy-covered abbey.

'Put her in with the others,' Mr Knight said, leaning out of the car. 'I hope you enjoy your stay here, my dear.' He smirked at her as he drove out.

The man in the black jumper motioned for Ann to head to the front door as he followed her. Absently wiping her feet on the welcome mat, Ann stepped into a cold hallway lined with doors on either side. 'In through that door,' the man said, pointing at one of them. 'Find an empty bed and get into it. No funny business.'

Ann opened the door and walked in, almost stubbing her toe on a table. The lights were switched off, with only a faint night light on the wall to help her see. The room was long and narrow, with a row of beds along either side. Each of the beds had what looked like a sleeping child in them, but she found one that looked empty and slowly made her way to it. She took her shoes off and slid under the covers, shivering slightly at the feel of the cold sheets.

'Hello,' Ann heard a quiet voice from nearby. 'Who are you?'

Ann sat up and squinted into the darkness. The girl in the bed next to hers was awake and watching her with curious eyes. 'I'm Ann,' she whispered. 'What's your name?'

'Molly,' the other girl whispered back in a broad Northern accent. 'You're not from here, are you?'

'I live up on the mountain,' Ann said. 'Up at the abbey with the Assassin Nuns.' She pulled her sheets off and swung her feet onto the floor. 'Where are we?'

'Don't do that!' the girl spoke urgently, motioning at Ann to get back under the covers. 'There's a nasty lady who comes in to check on us and she gets very upset if we aren't in bed after the lights go out.'

Ann jumped back under the sheets quickly, pulling them up to her chin. 'Is this a prison?' she asked. 'It feels an awful lot like one.'

'It's worse,' Molly replied. 'It's a factory.' She moved her pillow closer and rested her head on the edge of her bed. 'It's where they cut and polish precious stones.'

'I thought this was a school!' Ann exclaimed, almost forgetting to whisper. 'They told me that all the children were in a boarding school.'

'We do have lessons,' Molly said. 'We do English and maths and all of that. But that's only for an hour or two every morning. After that we go down to the mines.'

'Mines?' Ann's eyes grew wide. 'What? I didn't know you had mines anywhere near Pistachio!'

'Not near Pistachio,' Molly said, her voice dropping low. '*Under* Pistachio. There's a tunnel that runs underground, and the walls of it are filled with these stones that Mr Knight wants.'

'But isn't it really hard work?' Ann asked in surprise. 'Digging the jewels out of the walls? Why does he have the children doing it?'

'The walls of the tunnel are very narrow,' Molly explained. 'They're also crumbling, so the stones need to be pulled out carefully. I think Mr Knight's men tried getting them out on their own, but the walls started to collapse and they were afraid they'd lose all the jewels.' She stretched her hands out in the moonlight. 'We're small enough to get them out of the walls without damaging them,' she said. 'And that's why he has us here.'

'Precious stones,' Ann said, her eyes bright. 'I can't believe this is happening! I've always wanted to dig up treasure. This would be so exciting if we weren't being kept in this awful place.'

'It's not really that exciting,' Molly sounded unenthusiastic. 'We only go in for an hour at a time and it's really dark so you can't see much. You just have to pull out every stone you think could be a jewel and put it in your basket. It's only after you come out and go to the sorting room that you find out that most of your stones are pebbles and small rocks.'

'Have you pulled out anything big so far?' Ann asked. 'Any big shiny jewels?'

'They're not really shiny,' Molly replied. 'They look an awful lot like regular stones. I don't think they look like anything special until they get polished and cut upstairs. That's what all the big men do—they run the factory.'

'Haven't you tried running away?' Ann asked. 'It can't be that hard to sneak away in the night.'

'Mr Knight's men are always patrolling the roads around the factory,' Molly said, shrugging her shoulders. 'Someone tried to run away once, but I don't think he got very far.' She pulled the covers up to her chin like Ann. 'The girls are in this room,' she said. 'They keep the boys in the room down the hall. We all have our lessons together and then it's down the tunnel to pick stones after lunch.'

'Do your parents know what you're doing?' Ann asked. 'Everyone in town seems to think you're at some wonderful boarding school.'

'On the weekends we have an hour off to write letters,' Molly said. 'So that our parents think we're busy studying and playing that game that posh people play with the horses and kings that prance around a board.'

'Chess,' Ann corrected her absently.

'Aye, that,' Molly said. 'They check them before they get sent, so you can't put in anything that actually happens. I tried telling my mum once that I was getting tired of having pea soup for dinner, but they tore it up and made me write another one where I had to tell her all about the wonderful roast beef I'd just had.'

'What does he do with them?' Ann asked. 'With the stones, I mean.'

'Probably sells them,' Molly said. 'They get sent out in these special crates about this big.' She stretched her arms out to demonstrate. 'I reckon he's making a tidy sum with this.'

'But don't those stones actually belong to the town?' Ann asked.

'No one knew about it,' Molly said ruefully. 'But aye, I think they would belong to the town.'

'But that's terrible,' Ann said, sitting up again. 'The only reason he's pretending to be in charge of things at Pistachio is because he's stealing the jewels from under it!'

'What's Pistachio like now?' Molly asked wistfully. 'Isn't it almost time for the Winter Festival? My dad owns a grocery shop in the middle of Pistachio and it's always great fun to sit there and watch them set everything up.'

'You dad is Mr Morris?' Ann asked in surprise.

'He is!' Molly replied. 'We used to sit outside our shop during the festivals and watch them string the lights up around the town square.'

'I think Mr Knight's stopped all that,' Ann said. 'Nothing fun really happens there any longer. That's how I ended up here. I was at a book club with your parents and a few other people, and then—'

'Shhh,' Molly said, suddenly freezing. There was a faint sound of footsteps outside and both girls slipped back under their covers, pulling them up as high as they would go. The door slowly creaked open and Ann could see a woman stick her head in, holding a candle close to her face. In the flickering light, her head looked large and bug-like, with watchful eyes and a mean mouth.

The woman stood there for a few minutes, listening carefully to make sure all the girls were really asleep. Ann suddenly had a terrible itch in her leg, but tried her very best not to think about it, focusing instead on how many Huberts she could remember roosting in the pigeon loft at the abbey. Just when Ann thought she couldn't bear it any more, the woman left, closing the door firmly behind her. Ann waited for a few more seconds to make sure she wasn't coming back, and then reached down to scratch her ankle furiously.

'I think we should go to sleep now,' Molly whispered, still under her covers. 'The morning bell goes off pretty early and she doesn't like it if you start nodding off during breakfast.'

'What do you get for breakfast here?' Ann asked. 'At the abbey, Sister Ruth does French toast with bananas and maple syrup on Fridays.' She tried to remember what the delicious golden slices of bread tasted like but, much to her disappointment, found that she couldn't. 'It's probably not anything as nice here, is it?'

'Oh, it's always the same here,' Molly replied as she found a comfortable spot on her pillow. 'Porridge and an apple. You'll get used to it soon enough. We all have.' She stared at Ann in the dark, squinting at her face. 'Are you really from the abbey?' she asked curiously. 'My mum always said that those nuns wouldn't get off that mountain even if their abbey was on fire.'

'Yes, I am,' Ann said. 'I've been living there a few months now.'

'Do they know you're here?' Molly asked sleepily. 'Won't they wonder where you've gone to?

'I left them a note,' Ann said slowly. 'They know I went to Pistachio.'

However, for the very first time that day, she realized that it was a strong possibility that the nuns weren't going to come and get her after all.

18

While Ann was coming to terms with her terrible new life at Mr Knight's secret factory, back at the abbey on top of the mountain, the Assassin Nuns of Pistachio were having an early morning meeting.

'And you're sure she's gone?' the Reverend Mother asked, tapping her fingers on the kitchen table. 'She hasn't just wandered away for a walk or anything?' The nuns were gathered in the kitchen while Sister Ruth bustled around, trying to put together a quick breakfast. They had been jolted awake by the sound of the chapel bells ringing furiously and had soon discovered that Ann was missing.

'She's definitely gone,' Sister Sparkplug said, brushing her unruly hair out of her eyes. Vroom stood next to her, twitching slightly as though he knew something was wrong. 'She left a note and everything.'

'Bonjour! is the one who sees that she is missing,' Sister Pauline said excitedly. The guinea pig sat beside her with a tiny white nightcap on his head, nibbling on a piece of oatmeal that Sister Pauline had given him from her bowl. *'Tu es une petite bête merveilleuse et très intelligente, tu le sais ça?'* she said, stroking his back proudly. 'You are the best guinea pig in the whole world, yes you are!'

'That animal told you that Ann wasn't in her room?' Sister Beatrice asked disbelievingly. 'Nonsense.' She reached for a grape from the fruit basket and popped it into her mouth. 'He can barely run down your arm without getting confused.'

'No, he does not tell me,' replied Sister Pauline, mildly annoyed at her beloved pet's abilities being questioned. 'He runs into her room because the door is open and he waits there until I come to find him. When I go in, I see that she is missing and I run to the chapel to ring the bell.'

'What does the note say?' Sister Parsnip asked worriedly, stifling a yawn as she stirred her coffee. 'I really didn't think she was the sort of person who would run away in the middle of the night. Where did she go?'

'She hasn't actually run away,' Sister Ruth said, sitting down at the table with a cup of coffee. 'She's gone down to Pistachio to join some sort of revolt the townspeople are organizing.'

'Oh dear, that sounds most hazardous,' Sister Agnes said, twisting her long braid. It was much earlier than the nuns usually woke up, and they were all still dressed in their nightgowns. 'Why would she put herself in such terrible danger?'

'The note says that she'll only be gone for a few hours,' Sister Ruth said. 'But she's been away all night.' She stared at her coffee despondently. 'She should really have been back by now.' The toaster pinged in the background and she got up to butter some toast.

'Maybe she's just late,' Sister Beatrice said. 'That child is often late.'

'She did say yesterday that the town was in trouble,' the Reverend Mother said, looking at the others. 'Maybe she was right. Maybe something terrible happened to her.'

'What shall we do?' Sister Agnes wrung her hands in dismay. 'How far can we see from the edge of the mountain?'

'Just the tops of their roofs,' Sister Beatrice said. 'We're hardly going to find the child that way, unless she's perched on top somewhere.'

Sister Ruth returned to the table with scrambled eggs and orange juice, and the nuns sat together for a while in silence that was only punctuated by the clink of forks and the crunch of toast. 'You're absolutely certain she's gone,' the Reverend Mother said again suddenly. 'She isn't under the covers somewhere or curled up in the corner? She is a very small child, you know.'

'There is no one in that room,' Sister Ruth said with certainty. 'I've checked thoroughly. She's really gone.' The Reverend Mother lapsed back into silence, chewing her toast.

'Maybe we could send the pigeons down!' Sister Parsnip suggested. 'They'd be able to go down and have a look around and . . .' Her voice trailed away as she looked up to see the other nuns staring at her blankly.

'Oh, the Huberts can't talk,' she said apologetically. 'I always forget. Never mind me.'

'She might still come back,' Sister Agnes said unconvincingly.

'If she was coming back, she'd be here by now,' the Reverend Mother said. 'Something's definitely happened to that child.'

'Maybe it's for the best,' Sister Beatrice said. 'The abbey is no place for a child—I've always said that. Now we can just go back to the way things used to be without all this nonsense about visiting the town every week. Things can finally go back to normal.'

Sister Pauline, who was listening to this with growing surprise, couldn't control herself anymore. *'Quelle terrible idée !'* she burst out angrily, shaking a fist at Sister Beatrice. *'Mauvaise tête! Ronchon! Bien sûr qu'on doit aller la secourir. C'est notre petite Ann de l'abbaye!'* Sister Beatrice stared at her with a slack jaw, unsure how to react.

'English, please, Sister Pauline,' the Reverend Mother said patiently. 'Remember, we talked about this before.'

'I say of course we must go find her!' Sister Pauline looked earnestly at the other nuns. 'She is our little Ann from the abbey!' Bonjour! twitched his nose in approval as he sneakily reached for another piece of oatmeal from Sister Pauline's breakfast bowl. 'I also say that Sister Beatrice is a very grumpy woman,' Sister Pauline whispered to the Reverend Mother. 'But I am not sorry for saying the rude thing.'

The nuns stared at each other around the table, their breakfasts forgotten. 'I think Sister Pauline is right,' the Reverend Mother said finally. 'Ann is one of us and we can't let her be kidnapped and simply do nothing.'

'What can we do?' Sister Ruth said. 'I've been thinking and thinking and I'm at my wits' end. How are we going to find her?'

'There's only one real solution,' the Reverend Mother said slowly. 'I can't think of any other.' She paused and took a deep breath. 'I think we may have to go down to Pistachio and find her.' The nuns around the table gasped collectively—even Vroom whirred excitedly. 'Now, I know that the world is a terrible place and very bad things happen,' she continued hurriedly, before anyone could protest. 'But we can't let them take Ann away from us. She's a part of the abbey, isn't she?'

'But we haven't been off the mountain in more than ten years!' Sister Beatrice said incredulously. 'Are we really going to go now?'

'I suppose it all depends on whether we want to find her,' Sister Agnes said thoughtfully. 'I don't want to leave our safe spot up here in the abbey either, but I do want to make sure Ann is okay.'

'So do I,' Sister Sparkplug said. 'She's a brave little thing who's been helping out so much since she came to live here. We can't just leave her down there on her own.'

'That's right,' Sister Ruth said slowly. 'She's a little ray of sunshine, that one. I'm in.'

'But we don't know how to organize a rescue mission,' Sister Parsnip said dolefully. 'We don't have any weapons or training.' She absently pulled a tomato out of her pocket and bit into it like an apple. 'How are we going to rescue Ann from a man who appears to have taken over an entire town?'

'I'll be right back,' the Reverend Mother said, leaving the room.

'I hope she is well,' Sister Pauline said anxiously. Bonjour!, now full after his breakfast, crawled into her pocket for a nap.

'I'm going to start cooking,' Sister Ruth said after a quick glance at the clock. 'I think we could all do with an early lunch while we sit here worrying and deciding.'

The Reverend Mother reappeared carrying a few dusty folders from the office that she dropped on to the kitchen table in a pile. 'Records,' she explained. 'These are reports of the things that the old Assassin Nuns did and notes from all their missions. I thought we could use some inspiration.' The nuns grabbed a folder each and were soon engrossed in the exciting exploits of their predecessors.

'My word,' Sister Sparkplug said. 'They once caught a master burglar by hiding in the gardens all night in the cold carrying stun guns and a net until he crept in to steal a painting.'

'How did they not catch their death of cold?' Sister Beatrice shook her head in dismay. 'That sounds terribly hazardous.'

'Listen to this,' Sister Parsnip said, flipping through the pages. 'They invented a special sort of poison and used blow darts to knock out an entire army of attackers coming in from the south.'

'There are plenty of ideas in here,' the Reverend Mother said. 'We just need to come up with something we can put together to go to Pistachio and get rid of the man who's got Ann.'

'I've got heaps of useful weapons in the kitchen,' Sister Ruth said, pointing at the row of dishes hanging on the wall. She stopped and stared at the potatoes on the stove, bobbing up and down in the boiling water. 'Well get her back,' she said to herself. 'We'll get her back in time for tea.'

'Could we also collect all the torches we can find?' the Reverend Mother added. 'The sun's been setting earlier these days and you never know what's hiding in the dark.'

'Sister Sparkplug, do you think you could come up with something we could use to defend ourselves?' Sister Agnes asked, looking up from a folder with a photograph depicting the old Assassin Nuns wielding giant chainsaws.

'I'll see what I can do,' Sister Sparkplug said, pulling her glasses down over her eyes and tightening the leather strap around her head. 'Come on, Vroom, let's go make some weapons.'

***

As the afternoon progressed, the Assassin Nuns of Pistachio were hard at work. The kitchen had become the hub of it all, with rakes and spades piled up in one corner and Sister Agnes hard at work at the table, sewing special armoured vests to go over each of their habits. The Reverend Mother sat next to her, still poring over the old files while sipping on her fifth cup of tea that day.

'What about Sister Mildew?' asked Sister Agnes, putting a final stitch into place and trying a knot with a flourish. 'Is she coming?' She held up a finished vest and looked at it with a critical eye. A long pocket ran across the front of the vest, filled with Sister Parsnip's finest carrots and parsnips, ready to serve as as mini missiles for anyone who tried to get in their way. The side pockets were filled with carefully sealed bags of nettles, certain to injure the strongest of foes. The back of each vest had special pockets for each nun's individual weapons. 'I haven't made her a jacket yet,' she added. 'I can't imagine what she'd be able to do.'

'We can't leave her here alone,' the Reverend shook her head. 'Right now I'm more afraid of what she could accidentally do to the abbey when we're away than I am of anything down in Pistachio. In any case, she was one of the original Assassin Nuns! I'm sure there's some part of her that remembers how to fight.'

'I'll make her a vest too then,' Sister Agnes said, reaching out for her sewing box. 'Won't take me much time—I've done six of them already!'

'Oh, are those for us?' Sister Parsnip asked, coming in from the garden with a few more carrots. 'Here you go, Sister Agnes, that's more ammunition for you.' She picked a vest up and looked at it with great interest. 'These are wonderful!' she said. 'And the little missiles make a handy snack for when you're tired and feeling a little bit peckish.'

'I knew you'd like that, Sister Parsnip,' said Sister Agnes, smiling. 'Have you had a look at how Sister Sparkplug and Sister Pauline are doing in the workshop?'

'Plenty going on there!' Sister Parsnip answered brightly. 'They're making all kinds of brilliant things that would strike fear into the heart of anyone.' She jumped forward with a quick karate chop, narrowly missing Sister Agnes's head. 'Sorry,' she said, leaning forward to touch her toes. 'Just making sure I'm limber enough for the big fight.'

***

'Alright, my fellow nuns,' the Reverend Mother said as she stood in the garden facing the others, her habit billowing in the wind. She was wearing one of Sister Agnes's vests, with a 'Reverend Mother' badge Ann had made for her the previous week pinned to the front. Sister Sparkplug had made her a sword out of melted cutlery and an old thermometer, and the final product was an odd, somewhat formidable-looking weapon covered with fork tines and an embedded temperature bar that moved every time she swung it. 'Today we are no longer

the nuns who live on the mountain near Pistachio,' she said. 'We are the Assassin Nuns of Pistachio and we are on a mission.'

Sister Ruth nodded furiously, a spotless saucepan in each hand and her pockets full of whisks. Sister Parsnip stood beside her, carrying a spade and a rake, with several other gardening tools—including a length of hose—strapped to her back. Sister Agnes was still putting her vest on, a pile of wooden spoons piled up next to her feet.

'We're going out there for a reason,' the Reverend Mother continued. 'And we're doing it not just because Ann is there, but also because we are the Assassin Nuns, and this is what the Assassin Nuns do!'

'Yes!' Sister Sparkplug exclaimed excitedly. She stood beside Vroom, who had been given a few tweaks and now carried a torch and an electric lasso. Sister Pauline nodded furiously next to them, with Bonjour! on her shoulder. The guinea pig wore a tiny tinfoil helmet and held the smallest sword that Sister Sparkplug could make, while Sister Pauline brandished a hockey stick covered in typewriter keys and a bag of rotting fruit.

Bringing up the rear were Sister Beatrice and Sister Mildew, who didn't quite know what was going on, but was happy when she heard that she would be allowed to sing as much as she wanted once they got off the mountain. Sister Beatrice was still unsure about the whole situation, but had plenty of Holy Hand Sanitizer in her pockets, well prepared for any germs that might come her way.

'Are we ready?' Half a spoon fell off the Reverend Mother's sword and rolled down the mountain as she spoke, but she didn't notice. 'Let's go!' she bellowed.

As the nuns gingerly made their way down the mountain with their assortment of weapons, a gust of wind blew through the open kitchen window, depositing a few dried leaves next to a forgotten plate of cauliflower fritters and a bowl of untouched roast potatoes. For the very first time, these Assassin Nuns of Pistachio had found something more important to worry about than their lunch.

19

'I haven't been this far away from the abbey in fifteen years,' Sister Agnes whispered to Sister Parsnip as they stood outside the cornfield that Ann had passed through earlier on her way to town.

'How do you feel?' Sister Parsnip whispered back, clutching at her rake and peering suspiciously through the tall stalks. The nuns stood together, waiting, as Sister Agnes and the Reverend Mother went through the field to make sure it was all clear at the other end. They looked at each other in an uneasy silence, almost as if to reassure themselves that this was actually happening.

'I feel . . .' Sister Parsnip paused, furrowing her brow as she tried to find the right word. 'A bit nippy,' she said finally, rummaging through her shoulder bag for a bright yellow and black striped jumper that she pulled over her makeshift armour. 'That's better now,' she said, rubbing her hands together. 'I'm nice and toasty.'

Bonjour! twitched his nose in excitement as he perched on Sister Pauline's shoulder. As a guinea pig who was previously convinced that the abbey and its gardens made up the entire world, he was fascinated by all the endless sights and smells around him. '*Ça va petit bonhomme?*' Sister Pauline asked, pulling a piece of bread out of her pocket for him. 'Here is a little snack to keep you strong for the battle.'

The Reverend Mother burst out through the cornstalks, catching Sister Ruth unawares and almost losing an eye as a potato was hurled at her. 'Sorry,' Sister Ruth said sheepishly, putting away the carrot that she was about to throw next. 'I thought you were one of Mr Knight's men.'

'There are two of them out there,' the Reverend Mother said, rubbing her injured forehead and trying to catch her breath, as Sister Agnes stepped out of the cornstalks behind her. 'Two men are standing at the entrance to the town. I think they work for Mr Knight.' Sister Agnes nodded frantically in agreement.

'How do you know they work for Mr Knight?' Sister Sparkplug asked curiously, her eyes larger than usual behind her goggles. Vroom stood beside her, humming cheerfully.

'They were dressed in black,' the Reverend Mother said.

'And they wore black beanies,' Sister Agnes added. 'I think they had black shoes on, too.'

'There was definitely something villainous about them,' the Reverend Mother continued. 'Besides, one of them had a gun tucked into his belt. No regular villager would have a gun.'

'They were definitely henchmen,' Sister Agnes agreed.

'I have fired a gun before,' Sister Mildew said suddenly. 'It was very easy.' She smiled dreamily at the others. 'Pop, pop, pop.'

'Right,' said Sister Beatrice, tucking an errant piece of armour into place and stepping forward. 'Are we going to do this or are we going to stand here talking about it?'

'You two go that way,' the Reverend Mother said, gesturing at Sister Ruth and Sister Pauline. 'Take care of the man standing by the tree. Sister Agnes and I will do a quick check around this side of the road to make sure there aren't any others milling about.'

'I'll go the other way,' Sister Sparkplug said. 'Vroom and I will make sure there aren't more of them hiding around the other side.' She patted the robot broom on the back as they stepped into the cornfield together. 'Come on, old thing.'

'Where are we?' Sister Mildew asked. 'Is it time for hymns yet?' She looked expectantly at the others.

'Can someone stay here with Sister Mildew for now, please?' the Reverend Mother asked. 'Sister Beatrice? We'll come back and get you when we've made sure it's all clear.'

'What about the other man?' frowned Sister Parsnip. 'Didn't you say there were two?'

'I'm afraid I'm going to have to leave him in your capable hands,' the Reverend Mother said apologetically.

'If you have any trouble, I'm sure Sister Ruth or Sister Pauline can come help you.'

'You want me to go face a dangerous criminal alone?' Sister Parsnip began to look rather green. 'All on my own? I'm just a gardener, not a soldier!'

'You are an Assassin Nun,' the Reverend Mother smiled. 'You can do anything at all!'

'You must take Bonjour!,' Sister Pauline said, picking the guinea pig up and depositing him on Sister Parsnip's shoulder. 'He is very brave.'

'He's a guinea pig,' scoffed Sister Beatrice. 'Guinea pigs aren't brave.'

'Of course they are!' Sister Pauline exclaimed hotly, turning around to face Sister Beatrice. 'They are brave and—how do you say it—courageous and you always want one to be at your side when you are in the trouble.'

'I'd rather have a sword,' muttered Sister Beatrice, directing Sister Mildew away from the others and settling down under a tree next to her.

'Are we ready?' the Reverend Mother asked, gripping her sword with both hands.

'Yes!' the nuns replied in unison.

'Let's go,' the Reverend Mother said to Sister Agnes. 'We'll slip out from the other side of the field so those two out front don't see us.' She lifted her sword up in the air and turned to the other nuns. 'Go on, then,' she said. 'Go out there and be Assassin Nuns!'

Sister Pauline and Sister Ruth headed into the cornfield warily, while Sister Parsnip exchanged a panicked glance with Bonjour!. 'Okay,' she said to herself. 'Deep, even breaths. I can do this. I'm going to go out there and face that man and I'm not going to be afraid.' Bonjour! squeaked in agreement. She slowly made her way through the tall green stalks, brandishing her trusty gardening tools in sweaty palms.

When she got towards the end of the field, Sister Parsnip stopped and peered carefully through the cornstalks. The two men the Reverend Mother had told them about stood a few feet away, facing the town. Further along, she could see Sister Pauline and Sister Ruth peeking out as well.

'Okay, Sister Parsnip whispered to herself. 'This is it.' She took a deep breath, tugging her yellow and black striped jumper into place before running towards the first man with a loud cry, waving her weapons in the air.

Mr Knight's henchman turned around, dumbstruck, as what looked like a very large and angry bumblebee came charging at him, carrying a spear and a spade. He turned to his companion, but the other man was halfway down the road leading out of the town, with Sister Ruth and Sister Pauline hot in pursuit, pelting him with vegetables. Reaching for his gun, the henchman found himself grabbing a soft furry body instead. Bonjour! had decided to join in on the action and bit down hard as the man yelped in pain and then fell down in a heap as Sister Parsnip delivered a well-timed blow to the back of his head. 'Well, that was easy,' she said, dusting down the front of her habit and prodding at the man with her toe. 'He's knocked out nice and cold for now.'

'Well done!' The Reverend Mother beamed at Sister Parsnip, heading towards her with Sister Agnes. 'That was very impressive!'

'Oh, it was nothing,' Sister Parsnip said, secretly smiling to herself as she twirled the handle of her rake. 'I'm sure anyone could have done it.'

'Where's the other one?' Sister Agnes asked, cupping her hand over her eyes as she looked around.

Sister Pauline and Sister Ruth appeared from around the corner, dragging the second man by an arm each. 'He put up a bit of a fight,' Sister Ruth said, looking down ruefully at a broken frying pan in her other hand. 'I really liked this one. It was lovely for eggs.'

'We'll get you another one,' the Reverend Mother said, motioning them forward. 'Let's just get to Ann as soon as we can.' They tied the men up with some rope that Sister Agnes had remembered to bring along and left them propped up against a tree. 'That was excellent work, by the way,' she added, smiling broadly at the other nuns. 'It's almost like you were born to do it.'

The town loomed up ahead of them as the nuns carried on down the paved road that led into Pistachio, with Vroom trailing behind them, occasionally stopping to polish the cobblestones. 'I meant to program him to stop cleaning,' Sister Sparkplug said sheepishly. 'Forgot to clip that wire.'

The nuns stared at the houses and neat gardens around them as they entered the town. 'It's a lot smaller than I expected,' Sister Ruth said, poking at a hedge with her broken frying pan. 'I thought it would be more intimidating.'

'It's very . . . ordinary,' Sister Sparkplug agreed, her voice tinged with disappointment. 'Where are all the other henchmen?'

'What's that sound?' Sister Parsnip said, whirling around with her rake held high.

'It's just us!' Sister Beatrice cried, raising her arms up to shield herself from any potential rake-related injury as Sister Mildew looked up curiously at the houses. 'Put that thing away.'

The Reverend Mother led the way further into the deserted streets of Pistachio. 'I think there's someone in here,' she said to the others as they arrived at Old Joel's tiny corner shop. 'I'm going to pop in to see if anyone knows where Ann is,' she said, peering in through the window. She stepped through the door gingerly, with Sister Ruth behind her. 'Is anyone here?' the Reverend Mother asked in a loud voice. 'We only need directions.'

'Directions!' came a high-pitched squawk from the corner of the room as Zeus decided to make his presence known. Sister Ruth swung her frying pan around wildly, nearly knocking over a shelf of sweets.

'What on earth was that?' Sister Beatrice asked, sticking her head in through the door.

The Reverend Mother held her sword up as she slowly made her way to where Zeus' cage hung. 'It's a bird,' she said dismissively, putting her sword away. 'It's just a bird in a cage.'

'First it's guinea pigs and robot brooms and now it's talking parrots,' Sister Beatrice groaned. 'Whatever will be next?'

'Upon my word, it's the nuns!' Old Joel wheeled himself out of his customary spot in the shadows, a smile stretching across his wrinkled face. 'I didn't think I'd see any of you ever again.' He stretched his hand out to the Reverend Mother. 'Ever so pleased to meet you,' he said. 'I'm Old Joel.'

The Reverend Mother shook his hand and smiled. 'Hello, Old Joel,' she said. 'I'm the Reverend Mother and we're the Order of the Assassin Nuns.'

'I know who you are,' Old Joel chuckled. 'I used to see you lot all the time in the old days.' He pointed at the saddles on the wall. 'Those are from the horses the other nuns used.'

'The other nuns rode horses?' Sister Ruth asked disbelievingly.

'Aye,' Old Joel replied. 'I let them use my horses when their work took them out of town. They never really liked cars.'

Sister Ruth wrinkled her nose as she stared at the rows of saddles on the wall.

'If you ever need one of my horses, you just let me know,' Old Joel continued. 'They used to enjoy their little adventures with you.'

'Yes, of course,' the Reverend Mother said. 'But I doubt we'll be needing horses any time soon. We're just looking for a small girl, about this tall?' She stretched her hand out to demonstrate.

'Her name is Ann,' piped in Sister Ruth.

'Hair!' screeched Zeus. 'Hair! Hair! Hair!'

'Oh aye, I've seen her,' Old Joel said, wheeling towards the parrot's cage. 'Zeus here clearly remembers her too, don't you?'

'Hair!' Zeus repeated, hopping along his perch excitedly.

'Yes, she's a rather memorable child,' the Reverend Mother agreed, backing away from the cage. 'Do you happen to know where she is or if she's in trouble?'

'She should be over at the grocer's,' Old Joel replied. 'She's always there. Down the road right there and straight on. Big sign on the outside, you won't miss it.' He paused and lowered his voice. 'Watch out for the mayor's men, though,' he said. 'They don't like it when people poke around and ask questions.'

'That's what we're afraid happened to Ann,' the Reverend Mother exchanged an anxious glance with Sister Ruth. 'She does like to ask questions.' The Reverend Mother reached over and shook Old Joel's hand before heading for the door. 'Thank you for your help.'

'Don't forget to let me know if you ever need my horses,' Old Joel shouted as they left the shop.

'We're headed down this way,' the Reverend Mother said to the others, pointing at the road ahead. 'There's a grocer's nearby that she might be at.'

'We need to watch out for more henchmen,' Sister Ruth added, her eyes wide and solemn as they headed further into the town. 'The man in the shop told us that they're everywhere.' Her voice dropped into a whisper.

The nuns continued on their way in silence, occasionally punctuated by joyful buzzing from Vroom when he came across something to clean. The town was still oddly quiet, with no other traffic or passersby as far as they could see. 'That must be it,' Sister Sparkplug said, pointing at a shop ahead.

'I don't think it's open,' Sister Parsnip said, as they got closer. The shutters were drawn and a few wilted cabbage leaves lay discarded by the front step. She reached for a piece of paper nailed to the door. 'Closed until further notice by the mayor's office,' she read, and then looked up at the other nuns. 'Oh no.'

'He's got her,' Sister Ruth said miserably.

'This is terrible!' wailed Sister Pauline. 'What shall we do now?'

'We have to split up,' the Reverend Mother said. 'That's the only way we can do this.'

'Let's do it in pairs,' Sister Agnes proposed. 'Let's all pick different directions and meet back here in two hours.'

The Reverend Mother nodded. 'We have to spread out across the town and find Mr Knight before anything bad happens to Ann. Quick!' She pulled her sword out again and held it up.

'We're going to fix this,' Sister Ruth said, to no one in particular as the nuns disappeared down various paths and roads and into the heart of Pistachio.

20

Earlier that morning, while the Assassin Nuns of Pistachio were still deciding how to deal with the disappearance of their youngest member, Ann was woken up by the sound of a loud buzzer. She lay in bed, confused for a moment, until she heard muttered complaints as all the other girls woke up and started to get out of their beds. She sat up and rubbed her eyes, slowly realizing that everything that had happened wasn't a bad dream. A few of the girls shot Ann a curious glance, but most of them ignored her, almost as though they didn't really care about anything any longer.

'Good morning!' came a voice next to her, and Ann finally had a clearer look at her talkative neighbour from the previous night. Molly was short, with a snub nose and a smattering of freckles across her face. She had a smile much like Mrs Morris's and Ann knew instantly that they were going to get along just fine. 'Did you sleep okay?'

'I think I had strange dreams,' Ann said, as she tried to remember them. 'Something about running down a flight of stairs and a clown with a fruit basket.'

'Took me some time to get used to it here,' Molly said, her fingers flying as she tied her hair back into two neat braids. 'I used to have my own room at home and it's a bit hard getting used to so many people!'

Ann tried to tuck the stray stands of her hair back, but they insisted on popping out again after a few seconds. 'What happens now?' she asked.

'Breakfast,' Molly said, pulling on a pair of jeans and slipping a thick jumper on over her pyjama top. 'I can't be bothered to change,' she explained. 'We all have showers before we go to bed instead because of the dust from the mines.' She pointed at a queue of girls heading out the door. 'Off we go,' she said, tossing her duvet haphazardly over the top of her bed.

The girls stepped out of the room and into the hallway Ann remembered from the previous night. 'That's where the boys sleep,' Molly said, pointing to a door up ahead. The boys queued up alongside them as the children headed down the narrow passageway. 'I like your socks,' Molly said admiringly, looking down at Ann's striped feet. 'They remind me of twirly lollipops.'

'Thank you,' Ann said. 'Those are really the only kind I have. The nuns at my last abbey couldn't find any regular ones and bought me fifteen pairs of these instead.' Up ahead, the queue turned to the left and entered another room. The children poured in and sat down at two long tables that ran from one end of the room to the other. Molly found them two seats together and they watched as three of Mr Knight's men passed out a bowl of porridge and an apple to each child, while a fourth stood by the door with his arms crossed.

Ann lifted her spoon up and watched as the grey flavourless porridge trickled back down into her bowl. 'This looks like mud,' she said gloomily. 'Even Bonjour! has better food back at the abbey.'

'Who's Bonjour?' Molly asked, swallowing a mouthful of her breakfast quickly without tasting it.

'It's Bonjour! with an exclamation mark,' Ann explained. 'He's a guinea pig who belongs to one of the nuns, Sister Pauline.'

'We had guinea pigs once,' Molly said. 'My dad got us two of them. They weren't in the least bit interesting and just slept all day.'

'Oh, Bonjour! isn't anything like that!' Ann said. 'He knows French and can even play fetch. Sort of.'

'I can't speak French,' Molly said, making a face. 'That sounds like a pretty smart guinea pig.'

'I once knew a cat that could sing,' Ann said. 'When I was at the Abbey of Infinite Alarm, they had a pet cat who would try very hard to join in the evening hymns.'

'Your life sounds so exciting,' Molly said admiringly. 'I've never lived anywhere apart from here in Pistachio.'

'I do like going to new places and meeting new people all the time,' Ann said, twirling a strand of her hair. 'But what I'd like even more is to belong somewhere. I've never really belonged anywhere.'

'Maybe you could belong here,' Molly suggested, spinning her apple on the table. 'Pistachio could be your home.'

'I thought it could be,' Ann said, shaking her head. 'The nuns don't really want me, though. I left them a note telling them I was here and they haven't come to get me.' The fears that had been plaguing her all night started to slip out in a jumble of words. 'They know I'm here,' she said. 'But they're just too afraid to leave the mountain. They're just going to go ahead with their lives and things will go back to how they were before I got there. I bet that after a few weeks, they won't even remember who I was.' She lapsed into silence, studying her fingernails intently.

'I don't think anyone could forget you, Ann,' Molly said sweetly, smiling at her new friend. 'If we ever get out of here, I think you should come and live with me and my parents.'

The girls were interrupted by another bell signalling that breakfast was over, and the children lined up in orderly rows to rinse their bowls and pile them neatly on a wire rack next to the sink. 'Where do we go next?' Ann asked as she picked up her half-eaten breakfast and joined the queue.

'Fifteen minutes to wash up and then it's time for lessons with Miss Blank,' Molly said. 'She's the horrid woman who nearly caught us talking last night.' The girls shuffled along slowly down the room. 'That's Veronica,' Molly gestured at a girl ahead of them. 'She got too tall to fit in the tunnels, so now she has to spend her day with Miss Blank cleaning and packing the stones into cases. Imagine spending your entire day with that awful woman?' Molly shuddered. 'I'd rather live in the mines.' She pointed at another girl in the corner, smiling to herself. 'That's Jenny,' she said. 'She has an imaginary friend named Benedict that she won't stop talking about, so stay as far away from her as you can!'

'Who's that?' Ann asked, looking at one of the men guarding the door. He was big and broad-shouldered, with a tattoo of a snake curling out from under the sleeve of his black jumper. A narrow scar running across his eye gave him an especially dangerous look.

'One of the guards,' Molly said, fidgeting with one of her pigtails. 'He never says a word. I think I've heard some of the others call him Mike.'

'Mike's a terrible name for him,' Ann said, shaking her head. 'It sounds far too normal. No, let me think.' She scrunched her face up and thought for a few seconds. 'Arcady,' she said finally. 'Arcady the One-Eyed.' She smiled brightly at him, but he looked away, impassive. The two girls reached the head of the queue and washed their breakfast bowls out quickly. 'What are lessons with Miss Blank like?' Ann asked.

'Awful,' Molly rolled her eyes dramatically. 'I think you should tie your hair up nice and tight,' she said, passing Ann a handful of elastic bands from her pocket. 'Miss Blank made Susie Pearce cut all hers off because it was messy one day.' Molly pointed at a tall girl across the room whose short curly hair covered her head like a cap.

Ann tied her hair into a neat braid and tucked in all the stray strands. 'Any better?' she asked, turning her head so Molly could see.

'Oh, that's well neat!' Molly replied as they headed through the doors and back down the corridor again. 'You look like a completely different person!'

By the time the girls reached the classroom, Ann was starving. She'd been spoilt by Sister Ruth's wonderful breakfasts and a few mouthfuls of porridge had done nothing to whet her appetite. As she tried to settle in her seat and ignore the rumblings in her tummy, Miss Blank walked in and she forgot all about being hungry.

Miss Blank had the sort of face that made it look like she was always holding back a sneeze. She was dressed in a pair of black trousers and a severe white shirt with a collar so pointy that it looked like vampire fangs. She walked into the room and stared at the rows of children seated at the wooden desks and benches in front of her, tapping a wooden ruler impatiently against the side of her leg. 'I'd like to see everyone's homework from yesterday,' she said grimly. 'And remember, any mistakes and you will have twice the amount of homework for tomorrow.'

'That sounds terrible,' Ann whispered to Molly.

'You, over there!' Miss Blank said ominously, pointing at Ann and Molly. 'Fetch me your notebook.'

Molly scrambled around in her satchel and handed her book to Miss Blank, who turned the pages slowly, frowning over each word she read. 'Acceptable,' she said begrudgingly. 'But if your work isn't better tomorrow, you're going to get more homework anyway.' She turned to Ann and put her hand out. 'Let's see yours now,' she said.

'I only got here last night,' Ann said, standing up. 'I wasn't in class yesterday, so I don't have any homework.'

Miss Blank narrowed her eyes with displeasure. 'So you're the new girl,' she said. 'Why did you only get here now?'

'I'm from the abbey on the mountain,' Ann replied. 'I don't actually live in Pistachio. I was down in town for—'

'Excuses,' Miss Blank said sourly. 'All I hear are excuses.' She waved Ann back into her seat, and headed back to the blackboard at the front of the room.

The rest of the class was a bit of a blur as Ann, both hungry and sleepy, couldn't quite tell what Miss Blank was talking about. The entire lesson seemed to revolve around percentages, banks and savings accounts. Ann missed Sister Agnes's easy way of explaining various maths problems. She sat staring at the floor as she tried to remember what lessons were like at the abbey, until Molly gave her a sharp dig in the ribs. 'New girl,' she heard Miss Blank say sharply, 'I want you to summarize what I've been talking about.'

Ann stood up slowly, aware that everyone was looking at her. 'I don't know,' she said. 'I couldn't understand what you were saying.'

'Excuses!' Miss Blank shouted. 'If you aren't going to pay attention here, you might as well head straight to work instead.' She headed to the door and stuck her head out, and then stood aside as the large, quiet man who Ann had noticed at breakfast earlier stepped into the room. 'This one's ready to go down to the mines,' she said, pointing at Ann.

Ann left the room with him, turning around to look at Molly's concerned face before she stepped through the doors. The man in the black jumper was silent as they walked down the corridor. 'Hello,' Ann said tentatively, as they reached the end of the hallway and took a flight of stairs down into the basement. The man ignored her and continued to follow her down the stairs in complete silence. 'I heard your name's Mike, but I hope you don't mind if I call you Arcady,' she continued. 'It just feels like a much better name for you, don't you think?' Ann thought she saw his eyelid twitch, but she couldn't be sure. 'That's a really good scar, by the way. If I was ever going to have a scar, it would definitely be one like that.'

The basement was crammed with boxes and crates, along with an assortment of pickaxes, yellow hard hats and sieves. Ann stopped to pick up one of the hard hats and put it on her head. 'Is this what we wear in the tunnels?' she asked the newly named Arcady. He stopped and turned around, motioning her to follow him. 'I thought there would be some sort of breathing tube with it,' she continued, taking it off and examining it. 'How are we meant to breathe in the mines? I mean,

I'm sure it's not easy.' She put it down and continued to pick her way through the room. At the far end, another man was seated at a desk next to a large gaping hole in the wall that was illuminated by two large floodlights on stands. 'It can't be fun working down here,' Ann said to Arcady as they walked towards the desk. 'Do you ever forget what time of day it is?'

Arcady directed her towards the man at the desk, who pulled his headphones out and looked up in surprise. 'Take this one, please,' she heard Arcady say in heavily accented English. 'She talks so much.' He took a final look at her and sighed before leaving the room and heading back up to the hallway.

'Not another one of you lot.' The man at the desk stood up and walked over to Ann. 'You're early,' he said. 'Shouldn't you be at lessons?'

Ann shrugged. 'I got kicked out of lessons,' she said. 'They sent me here instead.'

'Okay,' the man said as he headed over to the pile of equipment in the corner. 'You'll need these before you go in there.' He handed her a pair of safety glasses, gloves and a pickaxe. 'Put them on now.' Ann strapped her hat on and slipped the glasses into place, imagining that she looked a bit like Sister Sparkplug. 'And that,' the man said, handing her a small light to strap onto her hard hat.

'What am I looking for?' Ann asked, pulling the gloves on. 'I'm new,' she explained. 'I haven't been down there before.' She peered into the hole, but couldn't see anything except for an endless tunnel illuminated by the bright floodlights.

'Just get in and grab all the stones you can find,' the man instructed. 'Don't waste time looking at them—you can do that later. You can't be in there pulling things out of the wall for too long or the whole thing starts to crumble.' He looked at his watch. 'I'll give you a shout when it's time to come out. No funny business.'

'I don't understand why you people say that all the time,' Ann said, walking towards the hole. 'Funny business. It makes you think of a clown company.' She readjusted her glasses and blinked. 'When I was at the Parish of Constant Bewilderment, they used to have this—'

'That's plenty of talk from you,' the man said, interrupting her. 'In you go.'

Ann took a deep breath and stepped in, switching on the light on her hard hat. She felt a little bit like an astronaut heading out to explore an alien planet and collect specimens, but unlike this imaginary astronaut, she didn't think she'd be able to go home when it was all over.

21

'I think I have found this place we are looking for,' Sister Pauline whispered excitedly. 'Mr Knight, I just see his face in the window now!' When the nuns had split up into pairs to look for Mr Knight, she and Sister Mildew headed down a narrow alley that had accidentally led them to his headquarters. There were two men standing outside the front door, and Sister Pauline had been waiting patiently for them to leave so she could try to sneak in. 'I am going now,' she whispered to Sister Mildew. 'You have to wait here until I come back, please.'

'No,' said Sister Mildew. 'I want to come, too.'

'Bonjour! will stay with you,' Sister Pauline said, as she placed him carefully in the palm of Sister Mildew's hand. 'See, I make him a small spear and tie it to his back so he can defend you.' She pointed at the sharpened end of a fork that had been strategically attached to Bonjour!'s armour.

'Hello, rat.' Sister Mildew smiled as she stroked the top of his head. 'Nice little rat.' Bonjour! looked affronted at being identified incorrectly, but decided he liked the petting enough to ignore it for now.

Sister Pauline tiptoed around the side of the building and waited for a few minutes until the men started to walk the other way. She slid out carefully, sticking to the shadows as she made her way to the main entrance.

'Where do you think you're going?' One of the men stepped out from behind a pillar and grabbed her arm.

'Get your hands off me!' Sister Pauline shouted, pummelling the man with the business end of her umbrella. *'Enlève tes sales pattes! Prends ça! Et ça! Grosse brute!'*

Bonjour! turned around, his nose twitching as he looked for his human. Catching sight of Sister Pauline wrestling with the guard, he raced forward, his tiny legs carrying him as fast as they could and sunk his teeth into the man's ankle. The man stumbled backwards, his eyes wide with disbelief and his arms flailing wildly as he tried to shake the guinea pig off his foot.

'Rat!' he shouted. 'There's a rat biting me!'

'That is not a rat!,' Sister Pauline said indignantly, pelting him with carrots from her belt. 'Why does everyone call him a rat? He is a noble guinea pig.' She flung her last vegetable at him with force and scowled.

'Where did it go?' Sister Mildew appeared, her arms outstretched as she looked for Bonjour!.

Sister Pauline watched in dismay as two more of Mr Knight's henchmen arrived, brandishing guns. 'Okay,' she said, putting her umbrella on the ground. 'Look, I am putting my weapon down.'

'That's your weapon?' one of the men asked, scratching his head. 'Really?'

'Come this way,' the other man said, gesturing towards the building with his gun. 'Mr Knight will want to see you. Don't try to run away.'

'This is exactly the place where I was going,' Sister Pauline retorted, reaching out to grab Sister Mildew's hand before she wandered away again. 'Why will I run away?'

***

'We've found nothing,' Sister Ruth announced miserably as she arrived back at the grocer's shop with Sister Agnes. Sister Parsnip and Sister Beatrice were sitting on the doorstep, with the poster from the door lying on the ground between them.

'There's no one around,' the Reverend Mother said, shaking her head. 'Sister Sparkplug and I knocked on doors as well, but no one answered.'

'Either this town is empty,' Sister Beatrice said, 'or they just don't want to talk to us. I think it's probably the latter.'

'Not a single henchman either,' Sister Agnes added.

'Sister Pauline isn't back,' Sister Parsnip said suddenly. 'Do you think she got caught?'

'Oh dear,' the Reverend Mother said. 'She's got Sister Mildew with her, so I really do hope not.'

'That's two more people to search for now,' Sister Beatrice said gloomily.

'Should we start pounding on people's doors and asking them to give us answers?' Sister Sparkplug asked. 'Vroom and I would be happy to do that.'

The Reverend Mother shook her head. 'No, I don't think they'll say—'

'A man!' Sister Ruth exclaimed, pointing at a figure walking up the road towards them with a bright red bicycle. 'There's a man over there!'

The Reverend Mother stepped forward as the man came closer. 'Hello,' she said loudly, waving her hand. 'Would you be able to help us?'

'Hello,' the man replied. He was young, with a worried face and an abundance of ginger hair. 'Oh my, are you really . . .' His voice trailed away as he stared at them with a wide grin. 'You're those nuns!' he said finally. 'Those nuns who don't leave their mountain at all!'

'Yes, we are,' the Reverend Mother said. 'We're looking for Mr Knight.'

'And why are you looking for Mr Knight?' he asked, his face suddenly impassive. 'He's not the sort of man you should be looking for.'

'He kidnapped our Ann!' Sister Ruth burst out. 'He has her somewhere here and we need to find her.'

'And his men may have two more of our friends,' Sister Agnes added.

'He needs to be stopped,' the Reverend Mother said. 'And we're going to stop him. We just need you to tell us where he—'

'I can take you there,' the man said, hopping onto his bicycle. 'Follow me.'

'Oh,' the Reverend Mother said, too surprised to say anything else.

'What's your name?' Sister Ruth asked.

'I'm Mr Allsop,' he said over his shoulder. 'Mr Knight arrested my wife and baby last night.'

***

'Why are you people here?' Mr Knight asked Sister Mildew as the two nuns stood before him in his office. He was sitting behind a large mahogany desk with a life-sized oil portrait of himself on the wall behind him. Sister Pauline found the effect oddly disturbing as she found herself looking at the painting every time he spoke instead of at his face. The other walls in the room were also lined with paintings, mostly of older men in uncomfortable suits.

'I used to paint once,' Sister Mildew said proudly. 'I had eight paintbrushes.' She held out three fingers.

'What?' Mr Knight looked confused.

'The paintings,' Sister Mildew said, pointing at the walls.

'Never mind the paintings,' Mr Knight said impatiently, getting up from behind his desk and walking over to them. 'Where are the other nuns and why are you here? Who sent you?'

Sister Mildew got up and walked over to a frame at the other end of the room. 'Hello,' she said brightly to the man in the picture.

Mr Knight stared after her in dismay. The interrogation wasn't going exactly as he'd planned. 'You!' he said angrily, pointing at Sister Pauline. 'You tell me what's going on over here.'

Sister Pauline glared at him from her chair as she cradled Bonjour! protectively in her arms. *'Toi, le méchant, pas beau, je te parle pas.'* She scowled, her brows knitted together in distaste.

'Where are my men?' he asked, pacing back and forth in front of her. 'What happened to them? And where are the rest of you?'

'Tu es bête et méchant et je ne te dirai rien du tout!' Sister Pauline said. She shot a glance at Sister Mildew, who was still continuing a cheerful conversation with the painting on the wall.

'Answer me!' thundered Mr Knight. 'I know you speak English. You live with those ridiculous old women on top of the mountain.'

'Ces vieilles femmes ridicules vont t'apprendre une bonne leçon!' Sister Pauline said, shaking her fist at him. Bonjour! took the opportunity to escape and made his way stealthily across the carpet and under the desk.

'What are you saying?!' shouted Mr Knight. 'WHAT IS HAPPENING?' He grabbed at his hair in frustration, his long, pale fingers clenching in agitation.

'Those ridiculous women, as you call them, are going to teach you a lesson,' Sister Pauline repeated. Bonjour! climbed up the leg of the desk and stood at the edge, the makeshift spear on his back poised and ready. 'And my guinea pig, he is going to make you scream.' She looked at Bonjour! and gave him a slight nod. Mr Knight turned around, startled, but he was too late. Bonjour! flew off the desk with a squeak, flinging himself at Mr Knight's leg with all his strength.

Mr Knight yelled in surprise and clutched at his leg in pain, a trickle of blood escaping from where Bonjour!'s spear pierced his skin. 'I'm going to get you for that, you little monster!' he yelled, reaching for his desk to grab something to throw at the guinea pig.

The door burst open at that moment and Sister Agnes and Sister Parsnip barged in, waving frying pans. 'There you are, you nasty man!' Sister Parsnip shouted, heading towards him with a cast-iron pan held high. 'We're going to make you sorry you ever messed with this town!'

Mr Knight limped towards the side door, trying to make a quick getaway, but he was hit in the face by his own portrait, which sent him reeling to the ground. Sister Mildew stood behind him, still holding the corners of the frame. 'I didn't like that painting,' she said to him as he lay dazed on the carpet. 'It was too big.'

'Sister Mildew!' Sister Agnes exclaimed. 'You did it!'

'Is it time for hymns now?' Sister Mildew asked hopefully, dropping the picture on Mr Knight and heading towards the other nuns.

'Yes, it is,' Sister Parsnip said, starting to laugh. 'It is indeed.'

Sister Pauline stepped out into the hallway, and straight into the middle of a full-blown fight between the nuns and Mr Knight's men. The Reverend Mother swung her sword around, knocking a few of them over, as Sister Ruth stood on top of a table, flinging cutlery at anyone who came near her. In the far corner of the room, Sister Sparkplug and Vroom were engaged in a fist fight with a burly bodyguard, who was losing quite badly.

'He's in there!' Sister Pauline announced. 'We got him! We got Mr Knight!'

Sister Sparkplug let out a cheer and waved a wooden spoon in the air. A few of Mr Knight's henchmen exchanged glances and tried to slip out, but a handful of well-aimed pieces from Sister Beatrice's armour put an end to any attempts at escape.

As Mr Allsop helped drag the unconscious men into one of the coatrooms, the nuns gathered together. 'We need to go and get Ann now,' the Reverend Mother said, her mouth pursed as she tried to push two pieces of her sword back in together. 'One of the men said she's in a house a few miles outside Pistachio.'

'How are we going to get all the way there?' Sister Agnes asked.

'We're going to borrow Old Joel's horses,' the Reverend Mother replied with a twinkle in her eyes. 'Just like the old Assassin Nuns used to.'

22

As she made her way down the inside of the tunnel, the first thing Ann noticed was the smell. There was a nasty, damp odour in the air, almost like decaying rubbish. The walls of the tunnel were covered with pockmarks and holes, where stones had previously been pulled out, and as she leaned forward to touch them, the stench grew stronger. A gust of wind blew through the tunnel suddenly, catching her unawares, and she nearly dropped her pickaxe in surprise. She peered into the darkness, hoping very much that something wasn't going to come charging out at her. 'Right,' she said to herself, her voice echoing along the tunnel. 'Where are those stones?'

Collecting stones from the tunnel was a lot harder than Ann had imagined. The walls of the tunnel were so crumbly that most of it started to collapse if she pulled at the stones too hard. As she held her breath, Ann used the pickaxe to help dislodge a particularly stubborn stone and then discovered a long, thin object buried with it. 'A toothbrush!' she exclaimed, pulling it out and holding it up to the light. Certain that she'd discovered the personal belongings of some sort of famous pirate or smuggler who had died while digging up some treasure, Ann put it in her pocket to investigate properly later.

After part of the wall started to collapse again, she stopped and sat cross-legged on the ground for a few minutes, staring into the blackness up ahead and wondering what the nuns at the abbey were up to. It was nearly lunchtime, so Sister Parsnip was possibly talking to her radishes while Sister Beatrice would be popping into the pigeon loft to scatter a handful of seeds. Ann imagined Sister Ruth setting the table and carrying a steaming bowl of soup to the table. Her stomach rumbled ever so slightly as she decided that it was probably butternut squash soup.

'Another one coming through!' she heard the man outside bellow. A few seconds later another figure stepped into the tunnel behind her, wearing an identical hard hat and gloves.

'Hello,' Ann said, glad to see someone else. 'How are you doing?'

'You're the girl who missed lessons,' Ann heard a boy's voice say. She walked towards him, squinting at the light from his hard hat. 'I'm Chris,' he said. 'Molly says you're from the abbey.'

'I am,' Ann said. 'My name's Ann.' She looked up at the walls of the tunnel. 'What's that terrible smell?'

'I don't really know,' Chris said. 'We're probably under the sewers of Pistachio.' He picked up his pickaxe and

chipped away at a piece of stubborn rock. 'But I suppose it's better in here than being out there with Miss Blank.'

They worked together in silence for a few minutes, with Ann holding her breath until she thought she would pass out. Another accidental swipe with the pickaxe led to her being showered with more of the smelly earth from the walls and she flung her pickaxe down in frustration. 'I hate this place,' she said.

'You'll get used to it,' Chris shrugged as he got down on his knees to sift through a pile of dirt.

'I don't want to get used to it,' Ann said firmly. 'I want to go home.'

'You there! Chatty one!' The man outside yelled again. 'Out!'

'You get to go up to the sorting room now,' Chris said, wiping his face with a muddy glove. 'Make sure you sit at the back.'

'I will,' Ann said, squeezing past him carefully in the narrow tunnel as she headed back outside. 'But why?'

'You'll see,' she heard Chris say as she stepped out into the room. The lights seemed oddly brighter after the dimmed floodlights underground, and Ann had to close her eyes for a few seconds so they didn't hurt.

'Get rid of the muddy boots and wash your hands,' the man said, pointing at a sink in the corner without looking at her. 'No one wants you tracking all that filth through the house.'

Ann stumbled towards the sink, splashing cold water on her face until she felt better. Stepping out of her boots, she walked back to the desk in her striped socks. 'Let's have a look at your stash,' the man said, leaning over Ann's basket for a better look. 'That's not good enough,' he said, shaking his head. 'You'll have to get more next time if you don't want to get into trouble with *her*.' He waved her towards the stairs. 'Go up,' he said. 'The sorting room is the first door to your left.'

Still squinting at the lights, Ann lugged her basket of rocks up the stairs. The last time she'd carried anything this heavy was when the Sisters of the Indeterminate Order had insisted on bringing their own mortar and pestle to a picnic to grind fresh peppercorns for their salad. Heading to the door, she spied a familiar face standing outside. 'Hello again,' she said to the man she had named Arcady, who took one look at her and closed his eyes in resignation.

The sorting room was filled with children sitting at tables with their baskets in front of them while two of Mr Knight's men kept an eye on them. As Ann watched, each child picked up a stone, wiped it carefully, looking at it from all angles, and then put it either in a small box on the table or a large bin next to them. Ann spied Molly waving at her from the back of the room and hurried over. 'Hello,' she said breathlessly, slipping into the seat beside her. 'Thanks for saving me a spot.'

'How was your first time in the mines?' Molly asked, closing one eye and staring at what looked like a smooth grey pebble with concentration. 'What did you think?'

'It's very horrible in there,' Ann said, blinking hard. 'I never want to go back. My eyes hurt when I got out.'

'Aye, it stings, doesn't it?' Molly nodded. 'Every time I step out of there, I have kitten eyes.' She scrunched her face up to demonstrate.

'I can still smell it,' Ann said, shaking her head from side to side in an attempt to dislodge the smell. 'That was terrible.'

'You'd better start working,' Molly whispered. 'You'll get into trouble if they think you're slacking.'

'How can you tell whether it's one of Mr Knight's precious stones or just a regular piece of rock?' Ann asked curiously, watching Molly make her way through her basket.

'There's a thin line of something shiny through the middle when you hold them up,' Molly explained, picking up a stone from the little box on her table. 'See?' Ann leaned forward and noticed a nearly invisible vein of iridescence running through the rock. 'Sometimes they give us toothbrushes to carefully brush the dirt off while we're still down in the tunnels and you can see it there.'

'Oh,' Ann said, slightly disappointed, remembering the mysterious toothbrush in her pocket. 'That's what it was.'

'This is unacceptable!' Ann heard Miss Blank's voice from the front of the room. 'This is not a good job at all.' She looked up to see Miss Blank berating Jenny, who Molly had pointed out to her earlier.

'She picks on everyone in the front rows,' Molly whispered. 'She's always going on about how they didn't find enough stones and how they should be working harder.' Ann nodded, remembering what the boy in the tunnel had told her.

Ann stared at her pile of stones and picked one up. 'Do you think if you kept going through the tunnel, you'd be able to dig yourself up in the middle of Pistachio?'

'I think those tunnels would collapse if you tried to dig your way out,' Molly said, shaking her head. 'They're not very sturdy.'

'There has to be a way out of here,' Ann insisted. 'We can't just stay here forever.'

'There really isn't,' Molly replied, looking around the room at Miss Blank and the other two men. 'There's always someone watching us.'

'There has to be a way,' Ann repeated, dropping a pebble into the bin. 'Didn't you say someone tried to escape before?'

'Bobby Davies,' Molly whispered. 'He made it as far as the main gate, but then one of those men swooped in and grabbed him before he could get through.' She gestured at a short red-haired boy in the corner. 'Ellie Potter tried to sneak out in the middle of the night as well,' she continued. 'But she bumped into Miss Blank in the hallway and all of us were woken up for a massive scolding.'

'I'll think of something,' Ann promised, twirling a misshapen rock on the table. 'I'll get us out of here.'

'You there!' Miss Blank spied Ann across the room. 'New girl who wasn't paying attention during lessons.' She made her way over to the table Ann was sitting at. 'Let's have a look at how you did today,' she said, tilting Ann's basket towards her. 'It's not good enough!' Miss Blank said coldly. 'You need to go back and get some more right now.'

'But I've just been in there,' Ann said, not wanting to go back into that terrible place again. 'I brought as much as I could—I really did.'

'Excuses!' thundered Miss Blank, 'Excuses yet again! Now you come with me, young lady. You're going back in there and not coming out until your basket is full.' Miss Blank marched her out of the room and down the stairs, muttering constantly.

The man behind the desk was talking to Arcady, but jumped up when they stepped into the basement. 'She's already been,' he said, pointing at Ann. 'She's been just now.'

'I don't care,' Miss Blank said. 'She's going in again.'

'No,' said Arcady suddenly, his deep voice booming. 'She is small. She should not go in there so much.' Ann looked up at him in surprise.

'Are you telling me how to do my job?' Miss Blank sounded incredulous. 'I'm going to speak to Mr Knight about your behaviour.' She reached for Ann again. 'Get moving!'

'No,' Arcady repeated. He stood up and headed towards Miss Blank. 'She will not go.'

'What do you mean, you great, big oaf of a man?' Miss Blank started to shout. 'Nobody says no to me. She can go back again and—' She was interrupted by the sound of a loud crash from upstairs. 'She's going back in.' Miss Blank continued, looking up at the ceiling with a frown on her face. 'And she's staying in there until she comes out with a basket that's full.' She let go of Ann's arm abruptly, shoving her to one side.

'Ow!' Ann said as she tripped over a crate and fell down, her knee slamming into the ground. As she sat there, clutching her leg, there was a second, louder crash from above. One of the floodlights wobbled and fell directly on top of Ann, knocking her down again.

Miss Blank put her hands on her hips. 'What on earth is happening up—'

'Hold it right there!' Much to her astonishment. Ann heard a familiar voice, as things started to swim before her eyes. She looked up in amazement to see the Reverend Mother coming down the stairs, brandishing an enormous, terrifying sword. She stepped forward, followed closely by the other nuns, waving spades, rakes and shovels threateningly. 'Step away from that girl this instant!' she thundered at a dumbstruck Miss Blank. 'That's our Ann and she's not going anywhere.'

23

When Ann woke up, she found herself back in her own bed with her books piled up on the table next to her. Someone—possibly Sister Mildew—had propped up a card with a Latin prayer printed on it. Ann sat up and gave her head a good rub. She could make out the faint shape of Sister Parsnip outside through the curtains, digging through the carrot patch, and somewhere in the distance Sister Agnes was shouting at the pigeons. Ann yawned, and then winced at a sharp twinge in her leg. Rolling her pyjamas up to inspect it, she was pleased to discover a violently purple bruise that stretched across her knee. She felt it looked rather like a badge of courage and hoped it would last a very, very long time.

'Ah, you're up then.' A smiling Sister Ruth stood in the doorway, carrying a heaped breakfast tray that smelled delicious and instantly made Ann remember how hungry she was.

'What happened?' Ann asked. 'How did I get back here?' She sat up and grinned widely as the tray was placed on her bedside table. The toast was slightly charred, just how she liked it, with streaky bacon, beans and two eggs beautifully sunny side up. 'The last thing I remember is all of you barging into the factory basement,' she said. 'But that can't be right, can it? Was it all a dream?'

'Don't be silly,' Sister Ruth said. 'Of course it wasn't a dream. There was a bit of an accident and you were knocked out just before that terrible woman made you crawl into that hole. We had to carry you home. It's lucky you weigh no more than a feather.'

'But where did . . .' Ann began, and then took a large bite of her eggs, the food muffling the rest of her question.

'We took out all four of the guards there,' Sister Ruth replied proudly. 'As well as that awful woman with the face like vinegar, the nasty thing. Sister Parsnip got her right in the face with a ripe turnip.'

'You actually left the abbey?' Ann looked incredulous. 'You fought?'

'Well, of course we did, dear,' Sister Ruth said cheerfully. 'We weren't going to let you go down there and have an adventure all by yourself, now were we? Ann shovelled a forkful of eggs into her mouth and shook her head in disbelief. 'We had a little help from that lovely Mr Allsop,' she continued. 'His wife—bless her—makes the most wonderful preserves. It's taken breakfast to a whole new level, it really has. Sister Mildew even forgot that we'd promised her she could lead the singing at prayers today.' Ann took another bite of her toast as she tried to put the pieces together. 'It's lovely jam, isn't it?' Sister Ruth continued. 'I had a nice big piece of—oh, can someone get that thing out of here before it ruins the carpet!' She looked on in frustration as Vroom made his way into the room, whirring in delight and trailing his usual stream of motor oil across the floor and rug.

'Vroom!' Ann jumped out of bed to hug the robot broom, nearly knocking her breakfast over. 'I never thought I'd see you again!'

Sister Sparkplug appeared hurriedly at the door, a frayed wire in one hand and a spanner in the other. 'Ann!' she exclaimed. 'How nice to see you up and about!' She stood in the doorway, smiling happily at her.

'The contraption, Sister Sparkplug,' Sister Ruth said in a sharp voice. 'The contraption is leaking all over the house again.'

'Oh dear, not again.' Sister Sparkplug tried to surreptitiously rub the oil stain into the floor with her shoe, earning her a scowl from Sister Ruth. 'Sorry about that. Come on, boy, let's go get this leakage issue sorted out.' She stopped at the door again to look at Ann. 'Just popped by to see how you were doing,' she said. 'Splendid to see you're all fine. I'll be back very soon!'

'That machine will drive me insane one of these days,' Sister Ruth said. 'Would you like anything more to eat?'

'I still don't understand,' Ann started, but was interrupted by the arrival of the rest of the nuns. Sister Beatrice shuffled in with a bunch of flowers in a vase, which she put on the table beside Ann's bed, smiling cheerfully. Sister Parsnip brought in a few freshly pulled carrots, which she was made to remove immediately when Sister Ruth noticed the shower of dirt on the floor.

'Ann!' Sister Pauline exclaimed with delight as she breezed in with Bonjour! on her shoulder. 'You are awake, this is so good!' The guinea pig ran down her arm and into Ann's waiting hand. 'Bonjour!, he helps rescue you too,' she said proudly. 'He fights this man all by himself with his little spear.'

'Bonjour! had a spear?' Ann asked, her eyes wide.

'Oh yes,' Sister Pauline said. 'He runs straight to this bad man and attacks.' She waved her arms in the air excitedly as she explained. 'He pulls his little spear and he—'

'He bit the man!' Sister Beatrice cut in. 'He actually bit him. We're living with a biting animal, sisters. This is worse than I'd imagined.'

The Reverend Mother and Sister Agnes walked in at that moment, animatedly discussing battle formations. 'The next time, we need to get them from all around,' Sister Agnes said, stretching her hands out to demonstrate. 'It's more likely to be a surprise that way.'

'Did you really come and rescue me?' Ann asked again.

The nuns stopped talking and looked at her. 'Of course we did!' Sister Agnes said. 'We got some horses from that lovely Old Joel and we got there as soon as we could.'

'Horses!' Ann said. 'You rode horses!' She stared at the nuns disbelievingly.

'Such a nice man,' Sister Agnes continued. 'He used to lend his horses to the older Assassin Nuns and said he'd be happy for us to have them anytime we wanted.'

'But what about all the terrible things that happen in the outside world?' Ann asked. 'All the germs and danger and shadows in the dark?'

'There isn't really much to be afraid of when you're carrying a giant sword,' the Reverend Mother said with a smile.

'You were so good with it,' Sister Parsnip said to the Reverend Mother. 'It's like you're a natural.'

'I'd never swung one before in my entire life,' the Reverend Mother said, miming the motions of a sword. 'I have no idea how that happened.'

'What happened to the other children?' Ann asked. 'What happened to that nasty Mr Knight?'

'Oh, we got him,' Sister Agnes said. 'And once we surrounded him with all our weapons, he was very quick to tell us exactly where you were.'

'His men were harder to get,' Sister Ruth admitted. 'I threw all my dishes at them, but they just bounced off those horrible big shoulders they have.'

'Bonjour!, he fights one all alone,' Sister Pauline repeated, smiling at her beloved guinea pig.

'The Reverend Mother knocked one out and Sister Sparkplug got another,' Sister Ruth continued. 'Right in the face!'

'How's Arcady?' Ann asked, suddenly concerned. 'He was trying to help me in the end. I hope he's okay.' She looked at the nuns anxiously.

'The big man with tattoos?' Sister Parsnip asked. 'He's fine. He was talking to the townspeople when we left. Telling them all about Mr Knight's nasty schemes.'

'I reprogrammed Vroom to turn him into a fighting machine,' Sister Sparkplug said proudly, sticking her head into the room. 'And he did so well until the wiring came loose, after which he started mopping the floor instead.'

'Sister Mildew actually knocked Mr Knight out with a painting,' Sister Agnes said with a laugh. 'Then she started singing, which startled some of the others so much that they got distracted and didn't notice us come up behind them with a shovel and a rolling pin.'

There was a sudden loud squeak and Ann leaned forward to see Sister Sparkplug push in an elaborate wooden structure in through the open door. 'It's a bookshelf,' she said, pushing her motorcycle glasses up over the top of her wimple. 'For your expanding collection. I noticed the shelf in your room is half full already, so I figured you'd need another soon.'

'So I'm staying here then?' Ann asked. 'You aren't sending me away?'

'Well, of course you're staying!' Sister Sparkplug and the Reverend Mother said in unison, as Ann started to smile.

Coming in to see what the fuss was all about, Sister Mildew walked over and peered through her moon-shaped glasses at Ann. 'She's awake!' she said happily. 'The elf is awake. Time for hymns.' Sister Beatrice appeared at her shoulder with a handful of jellybeans to distract her.

'The children all got back to their families fine,' the Reverend Mother said to Ann. 'Everyone's very happy to be back home. One of the girls, Molly, I think, wanted to know whether you were alright.'

'Molly's lovely!' Ann exclaimed. 'I'm so glad she got back to her family okay.'

'Mr Knight and the rest are locked up in the factory where they kept all of you,' Sister Parsnip said. 'We've notified the authorities and they're coming to take them away to the state prison as soon as they can.'

'Apparently they've been looking for him for quite a while now,' the Reverend Mother said, shaking her head. 'He's wanted on several charges, the horrible man.'

'Pistachio is back to the way it used to be,' Sister Ruth said with a smile. 'They were even talking about having one of their festivals next week to celebrate.' She stood up and glanced at the clock. 'Is anyone hungry?' she asked. 'I was thinking of putting something together for lunch.' She frowned as she tried to remember what was in the fridge. 'I could do a nice stir-fry with the leftover vegetables,' she said, mostly to herself. 'Ooh, or maybe some corned beef sandwiches—nice and easy.'

'I was talking to that lovely Mrs Argyll and she wants my cabbages for her stall,' said Sister Parsnip, almost beside herself with excitement. 'I've got to put more time into them from tomorrow—they're for real folk now, who appreciate good vegetables.'

'She's probably going to sell them to the farmers for the pigs,' muttered Sister Beatrice, but Sister Parsnip was too happy to care.

'I think maybe I should take Bonjour! out for a walk,' Sister Pauline said. 'He is a warrior now, so he must keep his energy.' She smiled fondly at the little guinea pig who was curled up on Ann's pillow.

'Sister Sparkplug!' Sister Ruth said with a tinge of annoyance. 'That pet broom of yours has made a terrible stain on the rug. How many times have I asked you to fix that problem with the leakage?'

'I have!' Sister Sparkplug protested. 'I fix him all the time! He just comes unfixed again, no matter what I do.'

'Why aren't we singing hymns?' Sister Mildew piped in. 'We sang so many yesterday and it was wonderful. Just wonderful.'

Ann listened to the nuns talking over each other and smiled as she stroked Bonjour! gently on his head. And for the first time in her life, she felt like she was truly at home.

Epilogue

As the months passed, the nuns decided to be more hands-on with what they now fondly referred to as 'their town'. The Reverend Mother and Sister Agnes helped reorganize the paperwork at the mayor's office—binning any laws that Mr Knight had passed during his time there. Sister Sparkplug helped get the library and playground running again and even built a few extra things for the children to play on, with Vroom by her side, constantly bumping into things.

Deciding that the townspeople needed a finer appreciation of food, Sister Ruth set up cookery demonstrations and helped reopen two restaurants, bringing in boxes of her decadent double chocolate muffins and passing out handfuls of rainbow-hued bonbons to anyone who stopped to talk to her. Sister Pauline and Bonjour! extended their morning walks to include the main street through Pistachio, as a gaggle of wide-eyed children followed them, fascinated by the odd pair they made. Sister Beatrice took a little more time to come around, but she was soon bringing in cuttings from some of her beloved rose bushes and planting them around Pistachio. Even old Sister Mildew started carefully making her way down the mountain and set about organizing a choir so that some of her favourite hymns could live on.

The mines were given to Pistachio and a new town committee was set up consisting of Mr and Mrs Morris, Mr and Mrs Skillet, and Farmer Argyll and his wife. Mrs Allsop was asked to join them, but she decided to wait until Emmy was older. Emmy, however, was not concerned with her mother's attentions and showed her displeasure by promptly learning how to walk.

The Summer and Winter Festivals were brought back with great enthusiasm and the nuns joined in this time, stuffing their faces with cotton candy and drinking large quantities of fizzy ginger beer until they needed to sit down.

As for Ann, she enrolled in the local school and found herself in the same class as Molly, and the two of them quickly became inseparable. Ann decided to work part-time at the newly reopened bookshop, but turned down the townspeople's offers to let her live with any of them. She spent her evenings with the nuns instead, joining them on their missions if she finished her homework on time.

And there were plenty of wonderful adventures to be had.

Acknowledgements

Niyati, Mimi and Nimmy, for getting me to turn a page-long story I wrote ages ago into something real. Especially Niyati, for not getting too frustrated with me when I forgot to reply to emails or lost my phone or got distracted in the middle of a conversation or saw something shiny.

Ruth, Pauline and everyone else whose identity I stole along the way.

Pauline, in particular, for all the French translations, squealing and motivational guinea pig picture spam at work. Bonjour! wouldn't have been Bonjour! without you.

My parents and Nihal, for reading all my drafts when I demanded feedback at unearthly hours, being excited about things from the other side of the world, and telling every single person they know about this book (whether they wanted to hear about it or not). Also, for being generally awesome.

And finally, Mark. For bacon sandwiches and shiny things and insisting that I sit down and write instead of playing “Call of Duty”. You’re my party tea.